THE PELLUCID WITCH

G. Owen Wears

Cover by Brian Essig-Peppard
Copy editing by Sabrina Smith

ISBN: 9798670344043

For the lunchtime crowd from high school.
Thank you for listening to my stories.

CONTENTS

ACKNOWLEDGEMENTS

I had forgotten about the man in the living armor. For the life of me I can't think why. He's certainly one of my more distinctive characters. Whatever the reason, it took a bit of effort on the part of my friend Jessica to convince me that I'd come up with the him sometime in the late 1990's. Once he had been jogged loose from my memory, the man in the living armor took on a life of his own. Not long after setting down the first installment of this story it began to grow, a bit like a fungus really, until it was a strapping little novella. I serialized it in my fantasy anthology "Exterus" and thought to leave it at that. No such luck. You see, very few people buy anthologies these days. This was a hard lesson that I learned after several years of putting money and effort into books that yielded very small returns. The crux of this lesson was that if I want to make any money from my writing I ought to do the popular thing and release full length novels.

Not long after I began work on the collected edition of "The Pellucid Witch," I discovered that I was thoroughly dissatisfied with it. I had managed to turn myself into a more-or-less decent writer in the years since I'd first begun serializing the story and the first few installments grated on me. Naturally I rewrote the whole thing. I had not intended to spend so much time on such a short novel, but it needed shoring up if it was going to go out in public. Ultimately, I'm glad I did. I'm also glad that the man in the living armor was knocked loose from my brain. Being able to bring him back into the world and share him with readers decades after his inception has been extremely rewarding.

G. Owen Wears
July - 2020

WORMROT

————•●•————

One

The wind dipped and eddied, swirling about the declivity where Krýl sat hunched, his arms propped on his knees. The sun on his face was hot, the wind drying the sweat that stood out on his bald scalp. Around him the shadows had begun to lengthen, stretching out long and lean as the sun dipped towards the red smudge that covered the western horizon.

Krýl watched the rock face before him, watched as a wind-spider the size of his hand moved from right to left. Its impossibly thin legs trailing in the breeze, it drifted closer, tumbling silently as the wind moved it. The fibers that sprouted from the center of its body gently prodded the surface ahead, mapping its course. Sensing the nearness of the wind-spider, Krýl's armor twitched. Slowly he eased himself back, away from the arachnid.

With a sudden jerk, the notched and pitted surface of

the armor extruded a tendril as fine and as sharp as the edge of a razor. It impaled the wind-spider, pinning it to the rock. The delicate creature's sensory fibers flailed as the tendril was withdrawn. A heartbeat later the armor closed around the wind-spider. Krýl could feel the eukaryotic shell begin to break down its prize, absorbing the scant nutrients. It did little to ease the hunger of the parasitic fungus that wrapped him like a second skin. Tugging at the base of his brain Krýl could feel it demanding to be fed. He pushed the urge away. It came back stronger, more insistent.

Krýl sighed, brushed aside his tattered cloak. Vents set vertically along his torso opened exposing sensory filaments. He felt the intake of air as the armor tasted the wind, scenting it like an aýr's hound. It took in pollen, dust, and pheromones. Through the fungoid shell Krýl could taste, smell, feel, and hear the little valley around him and the desert beyond. The copse of trees to his right were on the verge of bloom, their leaves having grown a reddish-purple. The predatory worms that slithered through their branches had raided a bird's nest and were gorging themselves. The armor urged Krýl to break his cover and to let it eat the worms. He held it in place, forcing the armor to remain stationary. If he exposed himself now, the girl was lost.

Krýl looked to the sky and took deep, slow breaths. Overhead, the clouds moved west to east, fleeing before the dark red smudge on the western horizon. The smudge sent up tendrils that seemed to grasp at the low hanging sun. It moved slowly, inexorably, towards the valley, towards Krýl and the others down below. He closed the cloak, tucked himself back behind the boulder.

To every side were splintered hunks of sand colored stone, their jagged edges jutting from the maroon and gold succulents scattered about the valley floor. The leafy, bulbous growths bent towards the west following the progress of the sun. Scattered about the defile stood clumps of stunted and bent trees, their leaves quaking in the breeze.

From the cluster of figures below there came a series of shouts and a peal of laughter that lasted far too long. Krýl felt his chest tighten.

Another braying laugh drifted up from the bowl of the valley, rebounding from the boulders. Krýl squinted against the glare of the sun, trying to count the number of bodies in the encampment. It was no good; he could see very little from this vantage. He should have circled to the north or the south before hunkering down. On his approach he had been over eager, the armor gnawing at the back of his mind, urging him to feed it. His judgment had been clouded and now he couldn't see how many men were clustered around that guttering little fire.

The laughter came again. Krýl knew it, hated it. He had laughed like that several times himself. It was the howl of a man in the throes of an ergoline induced hallucination.

The armor squirmed and Krýl cursed.

If the men below had taken it upon themselves to go for a trip then his job had just become exponentially more difficult. For that matter, what had they been taking and for how long? If he was lucky it would simply be bitterroot or blightfoot. If it was something more potent, say scarab or wormrot...

That decided it. He could not afford to wait any longer. The girl could not afford to wait any longer.

Krýl rose from his crouch and slunk around an out-cropping of rock that jutted to his left. The camp below was well situated, guarded on two sides by boulders. This, however, did not account for an assault from above.

Pausing, his back to the rock spur, Krýl drew a deep

breath. He concentrated, prodded at the armor. The chitin-ous plating that covered his right wrist began to stir. Then, abruptly, the pitted and gilled surface stretched and elon-gated, forming the rough semblance of a curved and ser-rated blade.

Krýl bent double, his breath coming in quick little gasps. He could feel the armor gnawing at him, siphoning off pro-teins, calcium, and amino acids. His already gaunt features contorted, the hollows around his eyes and cheeks growing darker.

Running his free hand over his bald scalp Krýl wiped away sweat. He cracked his neck, shook out his arms, then turned and slipped silently into the valley.

Two

It was not bitterroot or blightfoot the men had taken, nor was it scarab. Even without the aid of the armor Krýl could smell the wormrot from a dozen yards away. It stung his eyes and nose, made his stomach turn on its side. He wondered how the men had managed to grab the child with their minds fraying at the edges and their bodies reeking of death. Surely their approach would have been noticed, surely someone in the caravan would have raised the alarm. Yet here he was.

The mad laughter that had dogged Krýl's descent into the valley began to taper off. As he moved around the cluster of boulders, their surfaces still warm from the sun, the guf-faws degenerated into miasmic sniggering. Krýl hoped that whatever it was the men found so amusing continued to keep them occupied.

A few more steps, his footfalls nearly inaudible on the carpet of succulents, and Krýl stood behind the stones that bordered the southern end of the camp.

Raising his arms to shoulder height he again nudged the armor. The carapaced gauntlets that grew around his hands were rough and grooved, the fingers tapering to points. Krýl balled his hands into fists, shook off the pain of the armor consuming his body to fuel its own growth.

He was up the face of the boulder and bounding across its peak in the space of a single heartbeat. By the second he was over the side, his ragged cloak tailing in his wake. He caught a glimpse of six pairs of eyes all gone wide the instant before he struck. By the third heartbeat all was bloodshed and screaming.

Heedless of the fire he kicked and scattered, Krýl hacked his way into the circle of wormrotters. Sparks burst around his ankles, coruscating like fallen droplets of sunlight. His blade bit into the throat of the nearest man; another caught the curved length of chitin in the belly. The wet sound of viscera splashing across stone followed Krýl as he drove towards the third.

The laughter that had plagued him during his descent came again, this time relentless and deafening. Krýl could not tell from which direction it came; he simply turned upon the nearest wormrotter hoping he was the culprit.

The man was small, his wasted frame covered in scaly and cankerous growths. The noxious stench of the wormrot seeped from his pores, the blighting narcotic having eaten its way through the man's flesh. Krýl split his face from forehead to teeth. The wormrotter fell grinning, seemingly nonplussed.

More laughter.

Krýl turned towards the sound and was struck from behind. He staggered, blade upraised, and received a second blow, this time to the knee. Krýl fell hard on his left side. There was another burst of sparks as he rolled and crashed through the fire. The smoke that billowed from the oily wood choked him as he tried to draw a breath, the coals eating at the surface of the armor. He coughed and someone kicked him in the side.

Peering through the smoke and flames, Krýl finally located the source of the laughter. Standing over him, his face and nose a ruin of hanging flesh, was one of the largest men Krýl had ever seen. Clutched in his hands was a log half as long as he was tall. A rictus grin split the man's face, stretching his cheeks grotesquely out of true. What remained of his teeth could be seen all the way to the molars. In his eyes Krýl could see a need for stimulus. To this man Krýl's intrusion, the violence he had brought with him, was a delight.

Down came the log.

Krýl rolled to one side, trading the campfire for a heap of intestines. The man they belonged to lay where he had fallen, his face drawn up in a smile not unlike the one worn by the man with the log. Far from dead, the wormrotter was slowly, deliberately, feeding himself the coils of viscera.

"Tripe," gurgled the man. "Like the kind mother used to make."

Krýl pushed himself into a crouch as the giant's log careened towards his unarmored head. Obliged to again move, lest he be batter to death, Krýl threw himself forward. As he did he lashed out at the hands that clutched the log. Three fingers fell away and the trunk slipped from the wormrotter's suddenly diminished grasp. Now within his guard, Krýl rammed his blade into the giant's abdomen.

The giant grinned all the wider and wrapped his arms around Krýl. Crushing him to his chest, the wormrotter hissed, the man's corpse-breath rushing through rotted teeth and the ruin of his nose.

Krýl made a gagging noise.

With the giant's exhalation came a slick of blood that dribbled down his bearded chin. Krýl jammed his blade further into the man's abdomen. The giant's eyes glazed and his grip faltered. Krýl pushed himself free and the giant slumped to the ground, curling into a ball with his face in the dirt.

Krýl heaved a sigh, staggered to his feet, then froze.

How many had that been? Krýl counted backwards in his head. He had killed four of the six. The two remaining wormrotters made their presence known by hissing at Krýl like a pair of pit vipers

One to his right, the other to his left. Krýl did his best to watch them both at the same time. The wormrotters gawked at him, their faces awash with a mixture of euphoria and cruel purpose. Hands that had been atrophied and bent into claws twitched. Flesh, loose and beginning to slough from the bone, quivered in anticipation of relief from the excess of energy brought on by the narcotic salts.

Krýl braced himself. If the two wormrotters had any sense of how to conduct themselves in a fight they would attack simultaneously. With their lack of regard for their own wellbeing they might be able to break past Krýl's guard. He decided not to give them the chance. Moving to his left, he swung low.

As he passed, the right leg of the first wormrotter came off at the knee. The man toppled. Krýl turned about and drove towards the remaining wormrotter. His swing went wide as the man tackled him about the middle.

Driven backwards, his feet going out from under him, Krýl hit the carpet of succulents with a grunt. He pushed at the wormrotter, cursed, tried to knee him in the groin. The man atop him mimicked his exclamation then sniggered.

Hooting and gibbering, the wormrotter grabbed at Krýl's chest. With his bare hands he tried to tear away the fungoid armor. All he received for his efforts were bloodied fingers and the loss of several nails.

Krýl reached up to the man's neck, dug in his claws, and squeezed. The wormrotter left off tearing at the armor and clutched his throat. Blood ran between his fingers, his mouth working soundlessly. Krýl heaved the man to one side.

Brushing soot and grime from chest and thighs, Krýl did a recount of the casualties. Four of the wormrotters were dead, two lay wounded. One of the wounded was crawling towards him, the same manic grin he had worn through the whole of their exchange pulling at his face. As he moved, the stump of his leg left a trail of crimson in the dirt.

"The eyes…" said the wormrotter in a voice like broken glass. "One blue, one green…plucked them out…"

Krýl rammed his blade through the back of the man's skull. His gibbering stopped.

Krýl tugged at the serrated length of chitin. It remained where it was.

"Fuck."

Krýl set his foot on the wormrotter's neck and pulled. Grating along bone, the blade came free with a wet sucking noise.

Trying his best to ignore the smell that still lingered in the air, Krýl scanned the campsite. The girl was nowhere to be seen. There were the corpses of the wormrotters, a scattering of baggage, the remains of the fire; nothing more. Krýl's heart sank. If they had dumped her somewhere between the caravan and here he would have to follow their backtrail until—

A sound like the roar of a bonfire drew Krýl's attention up and away from the campsite. He raised his eyes to what remained of the horizon.

As Krýl watched, the swirling mass of red that had hung

low in the western sky rose higher. It grasped at the last of the daylight, tendrils turning like dervishes. By Krýl's reckoning he had an hour, perhaps less.

"No," said a strangled voice from opposite the scattered remains of the fire. Krýl turned from the oncoming storm. "No," said the voice again. "Not like mother's at all."

Krýl stepped around first one body then another. He squatted beside the man whose guts he had strewn across the campsite. The grin had vanished from the wormrotter's face. In its place was a frown smeared brown and red. The length of intestine he held in his blood-slick fingers oozed and stank.

"Not like mother's at all."

Krýl turned his head to one side. "Mother's...?"

"Tripe," said the wormrotter. "Mother always made it best. Not like this swill."

Krýl suppressed his urge to vomit or flee. He raised his hand and flicked the wormrotter in the forehead. "Where is she?"

"Can't get anything good to eat in this country," said the wormrotter. He spat to one side.

"The girl you took," said Krýl, "tell me where she is."

"Worm-salts, yes," said the wormrotter, "you can find those. But a good supper? Never."

Krýl hit the man hard in the side of the head. The glazed eyes of the wormrotter became suddenly fierce and he made as though to rise. The wound in his abdomen thwarted his attempt at violence and he fell to his side.

"Where is she?"

"No food," said the man. His idiot stare returned, passed through the armored man hovering over him. "Not in this country."

Krýl drew back his fist for a second blow then stopped.

He followed the man's line of sight, his arm sinking slowly to his sides.

Leaving the wormrotter where he lay, Krýl stepped over the collection of corpses and approached the heap of luggage that stood off to one side. When he reached the pile of torn and rotting kit he raised one carapaced hand, then stopped. His heart sank. With the tip of the bladed extrusion Krýl lifted aside the folds of the blanket that had been tossed over the pile.

The armor, its nagging having grown silent during the long minutes of bloodshed, again began to mutter. It yammered to be fed, the thing under the blanket causing it to seethe. Krýl shoved it aside and gathered the little bundle into his arms. He tucked a stray lock of blonde hair back into place, then took several steps to the east.

The nagging urge came again, the armor prodding him, filling the back of his mind with promises of chemical rewards. Krýl snorted and moved towards one of the dead men. At the stench of the wormrotter the armor balked. With a grunt Krýl turned back towards the east and away from the camp.

A tinkling sound, like glass chimes in a breeze, made him raise his head. Krýl saw the first lucent fingers of the storm begin to swallow the sun. Shards of airborne crystal danced around the boulders that loomed over the campsite, filling every crevice and hollow. They scurried along the ground, catching the dying light as they fled before the wind. Soon the shards would cover the valley, stripping it bare, killing everything they touched.

Krýl clenched his jaw and waited for the eukaryotic shell's inevitable response.

As the armor closed around his face and head, Krýl tried to suppress a scream. He could feel the eukaryotic shell digging into him, yet again siphoning off the raw material needed to fuel its growth. He cursed the approaching storm and his need for the helmet and faceplate. But were he to forgo the carapace the oncoming squall would strip the flesh from his bones.

The armor continued cry out for the contents of the bundle; for base components, the raw materials it needed. Again Krýl refused. Putting his back to the onrushing wall of crystal, he made his way from the camp and towards the rim of the valley.

Three

The man with the silver tongue smiled showing silver gums and silver teeth. He turned his head to the left, to the right, the sun reflecting from his incisors. Krýl waited for the man to speak. At last he cleared his throat and said, "Haven't got a problem with deviants, have you?"

Krýl said that he did not.

"Good." The man with the silver tongue continued to grin. "You'll be riding with several of them."

Krýl nodded.

In the distance a locust began to drone. The dry clatter was taken up by another locust, then another.

The man with the silver tongue gave him a sordid little look. "Nothing to say? No questions?"

Krýl shook his head, scratched at one cheek, and looked off to the side. He did not care if he rode with men or with deviants. It may have been understandable that the man with the silver tongue needed to ask; that was part of his job. But Krýl did not care one way or the other. In his experience it did not matter what species one was dealing with. In every group there were vermin. The number of limbs or eyes had nothing to do with how they conducted themselves.

"Come," said the man with the silver tongue, turning from the market square.

Krýl followed a few paces behind, his kit slung over one shoulder, his hood up. The man with the silver tongue walked with a scampering shuffle, his feet hardly leaving the cobbles. Gray and black damask swished about his ankles, his voluminous sleeves trailing in the dirt. Krýl wondered how he could wear such a heavy robe when the sun was so high and bright. Around them the city stood like a ramshackle maze baking in the heat, its alleys spiraling out, out towards the desert.

Between mud-brick buildings and through dusty streets Krýl walked behind the little man. The chattering of locusts was all around them; reverberating from the sides of buildings, hanging suspended in the air. The insects clung to rooftops and walls, making whole buildings appear to move and crawl. Krýl and the man with the silver tongue walked in a zig-zag trying their best to keep from crushing them underfoot.

Tucked away in alcoves along cramped side streets sat merchants and slavers, tradesmen and hawkers. They watched as Krýl and as the man with the silver tongue passed by, silent and still. Women in homespun burqas milled about wells capped with eight-sided stones, whispering to one another. Men in kufiyahs sat beneath threadbare awnings sipping tea spiced with blackleaf and katcha. All pretended not to notice the insects.

"How much further?"

"Not much," said the man with the silver tongue. "Not much."

Krýl wiped his sleeve across his forehead, drew a hand through his beard. It came back damp with sweat.

"How much is not much?"

The man with the silver tongue gave him a wink.

Krýl scuffed to a halt.

"I've changed my mind."

The man with the silver tongue stopped and turned. "Oh, what a pity. We're nearly there. The rendezvous is just the other side of these tenements. It is, of course, your choice if you wish to seek employment elsewhere. Unfortunately, this is the last caravan that will be leaving before the heat of summer makes passage through the Red Lands impossible. You will have to abide here, in the city, until the rains come again. That will be a very long time."

The droning of the locusts began to fade, silence moving in a wave across the city.

Krýl watched the man with the silver tongue, listened as the sound of the locusts faded. It could be true, what the man said—he might be left alone, in a city that was not known for its mercies or kind treatment of strangers.

With a sigh Krýl indicated that the man with the silver tongue should lead on. The little fellow smiled, pinching his silver tongue between his silver teeth. "Good," he said. "Good."

Another two blocks and the man with the silver tongue was as good as his word. The caravan stood at the periphery of a sprawling market square, its paving cracked and buckling. Counting the two dozen wagons, the four score head of hýthric, the hundred merchants and guardsmen Krýl breathed more easily.

Without breaking stride the man with the silver tongue made his way to a group of soldiers clustered in the shade of a wagon. He was greeted with a few cursory nods. Krýl approached slowly, his pace as nonchalant as he could manage.

"I've brought you a tenth man," said the man with the

silver tongue, "and within your asking price."

The bearded man to which Krýl's guide spoke said nothing, simply continued buckling the straps on the side of a wagon. As the canvas awning was winched taught, he twitched one of the withered little arms that depended from his shoulder. With a three fingered hand he scratched at a pair of mismatched horns that grew from his mop of black hair. Turning indigo eyes on Krýl, the deviant looked him up and down.

"Name?"

"Krýl."

"I'm Baalt. You ever traveled the wastes?"

Krýl nodded. "I've worked caravans for the last six years."

"You look like you were a regular before you went independent. You walk like a soldier. Infantry or cavalry?"

"Both, but never a regular."

Baalt raised an eyebrow. "Career merc?"

Krýl nodded again.

Another of Baalt's extra limbs flicked a locust from his should, then raised itself and pointed. "I'd give you a speech about keeping at your post and following orders, but there's no need. Once we get into the waste the only way you live is if you stay with the caravan. If you feel the need to disobey orders, I'll just leave you behind. If you dip into a pouch of scarab or wormrot, that'll get you left behind as well."

"Understood." Krýl made a concerted effort to keep his hand from straying to the pouch inside his tunic.

"Good."

Baalt turned to the scaled man that stood beside him. "This is Xhith; you'll report directly to him. Don't come to me unless he's dead. Obey orders and you'll get your pay like everyone else."

Krýl looked up at Xhith, tried his best not to stare, and failed miserably. The man was easily a head taller than the others, his features minimal save for deeply sunken cheeks, temples, and eyes. Gray-black scales and spiked ridges along his head and neck gave him the look of a sand-adder. Of all the soldiers clustered in the shade of the wagons, he alone seemed unperturbed by the heat. The man was a full deviant, adapted to the wastes and the searing desert sun.

"We'll be gone by sundown," said Baalt. "Till then get some rest and help yourself to some food. We've a goat roasting at the back of the wagon train. Xhith will show you." As he turned to go, his progress was stayed by a small sound from the man with the silver tongue.

Baalt grunted, dug into a pouch at his belt, and produced a handful of coins. He counted out eight. The man with the silver tongue grinned.

Four

Outside the cave the wind moaned like a bereft mother. It drove tiny particles of red crystal against the rocks that over-hung the small crevasse. Eddies of razor keen flecks swirled in the entrance to the cave, ran in runnels along the floor. They collected about the feet of the men huddled against the far wall. Krýl watched the piles grow, granule by granule; watched them grow until they had covered the first of the corpses, then the second.

Krýl tried to sleep, but could not. Krýl tried to push aside his nagging thirst, but could not. Outside the cave the wind was constant, the pitch rising and falling, rising and falling.

"It was nine…"

"Stop."

Krýl glanced up, shook his head, and closed his eyes. He

heard the others mutter, shift position.

"Nine days into the Red Lands."

"Be silent."

"They came at us out of the setting sun, used it to cover their approach."

"We know. We were there."

Krýl tried to block out the words. He had heard it a dozen times before. A hundred.

"The men on the right flank didn't have a chance."

"We were there."

"By the time we spurred ourselves around to meet them it was too late. The caravan broke, scattered!"

"We know, we lived it!"

"There was no point in their engaging us. They did it anyway. Broke us apart, picked us off…"

Krýl gritted his teeth, tried not to add his own commentary to the running tally of miseries and failures.

"By the time we'd regrouped it was over and done with. The caravan was lost. It was lost…"

"Who do you think you're talking to? Be silent."

"Lost…"

"Be silent!"

There was the sound of a stone striking flesh. It was followed by a whimper and a sob. Krýl looked to where the speaker had tucked himself into a fetal ball. Beside him, Baalt lay propped against a boulder. He twitched, one of his extra limbs spasming. The crystals that had built up around his feet and legs fell away. Krýl could see that only one of Baalt's horns remained. The flesh around the space where his left eye should have been was crusted over with crystal so that the wound glittered in the low light. Krýl looked down at his own feet. Baalt groaned and rolled to one side.

"It was nine…"

"Stop!"

"Nine days into the Red Lands."

Over the wind and the tinkling crystals Krýl heard someone rise and shuffle to where the speaker sat. There came the sound of blows.

Again Baalt stirred, changed position. Krýl lifted the scarf from about his nose and mouth. He shook bits of crystal from his beard and unstuck his tongue from the roof of his mouth.

"That's enough."

Xhith turned from the man he had thumped to glare at Krýl.

"He's dead."

Xhith grunted, bent towards the slumped figure. "No. Still breathing. Too bad."

Krýl shrugged, sending crystalline shards to the floor in a tiny cascade. "I'm going to go further in."

Xhith regarded him, nictitating membranes flicking back and forth over his eyes. "Khant went yesterday. He did not return. If you go, you will not return. Better to stay and let us drink your blood after you are dead."

"Drink Baalt's," said Krýl, rising stiffly to crouch against the cave's low ceiling. In the pale glow that bled through the cave mouth he could see Xhith stiffen.

"Go into the cave," said the deviant. "Go or I will not wait for you to die before I drink you."

Krýl turned his back on the deviant, the small cluster of survivors. He pulled a phosphorous torch from his pack, lit it, and moved into the gap between the rocks at the back of the cave.

The sound of the wind and the jingle of crystal was gone after a dozen steps. The sweltering heat of the desert dissipated, replaced by cool, dry air. In the light of his phosphorous torch Krýl could see only pale rock, shot through with veins of carmine and opalescent crystal. On the floor layers of dust and sand sparkled and winked as he moved. There were footprints in the dust; Khant's or maybe the man that had gone before him. Krýl followed them until the dust gave way to a carpet of sheer and jagged stones. The stones gave way to boulders, the boulders to slabs of bedrock that pressed in on one another. Krýl passed over and around, squeezing through interstices barely wide enough to fit his shoulders. He slithered on his belly, his torch held before him. He shimmied up precipitous rock faces and down precipitous slopes. Around him the cave was silent; the air was still. The hiss and gutter of his torch was the only sound save for his breathing and the scrape and shuffle of his feet.

Krýl rested when the strain of climbing became too much, counting off the minutes in his head, trying to keep track of the waning day. Eventually he gave up on counting. Time did not matter, not here, under the earth. In this place there was only the dark and the stones.

Krýl let his thirst drive him; allowed it to claw at him, his breath like windblown sand against his throat. If he could have outrun his thirst he would have done so, gladly throwing himself into the timeless dark or out into the storm. But there was no water outside the cave, only ravening particles of crystal. They would take his flesh, score his bones. No, if there was water it would be here, buried deep, deep within the earth.

The phosphorous torch guttered, spat, guttered again. Krýl shook it. The torch responded by dimming, fading, dying. Krýl slumped against the wall of the cave, drew breath, and screamed. When the echoes had faded he dropped his head into his hands.

The sound of his own blood and the thud of his heart

filled his ears. Krýl listened to his body, waited for the sounds of life to ebb, then fade. They did not. Instead the darkness around him seemed to draw breath. It bore down on him, pulsed in time to his own heartbeat. He opened his mouth to scream again, but found that he could not.

Five

He woke to nothingness. For a moment Krýl thought he was blind, thought he was dead, thought that the earth had risen up and swallowed him alive. He began to hyperventilate. Then he remembered; remembered Xhith, and Baalt, and the crystalline storm. Swallowing what felt like a mouthful of sand he fought back his panic, slowed his breathing.

Krýl sat up and listened. He brushed a hand along the cave wall. Under his fingertips the stone was smooth and cool. In his ears was the steady trickle of water.

Krýl started.

Straining to hear over his own pulse, he leaned forward, nearly fell, caught himself.

At first he was sure he had imagined it, but the noise persisted. It was a trickle accompanied by a slow drip, drip. Cautiously he moved forward, feeling ahead of himself, moving in the direction of the sound.

The noise increased. It was unmistakable, the sound of water running over stone. Krýl surged forward. He was rewarded by a sharp crack to the head. He teetered for a moment, watching as stars danced across his vision. When he had regained his composure he again moved towards the drip and trickle until, at last, his hand touched something wet.

Bending down, pressing his lips to the stone, Krýl drank. He sucked at the runnel of water, inhaling it. He waited, pressed his lips to the rock, and sucked again. He did this over and over while silent tears ran from his eyes. When at last the edge had been taken from his thirst he sat upright and wiped at his cheeks.

"More," he said, and heard his own voice come back to him. Krýl laughed, then began to drag himself along the trickle of water further into the depths of the cave.

Krýl had grown used to ignoring his eyes and what they were not telling him. But, after long minutes of sitting and staring, he was at last able to divine the dim glow that rose from the pool ahead. He blinked, rubbed at his eyes.

The cavern was small, no more than twice as long as a man is tall. At its center, the pool glowed a faint whitish blue. Rising from its edge grew viridescent moss and pale lichen. The glow of the pool was matched by the ghostly shimmer of hundreds of filaments that dangled from the ceiling. These swayed in time with Krýl's breath, the hair-thin tendrils moving in waves.

Heedless of the filaments overhead and the moss under-foot, Krýl stumbled down the incline that lead into the cavern. Splashing into the pool, Krýl dunked his face and began to drink. He came up laughing and spluttering, wiping at the droplets that clouded his vision.

As his eyes cleared, his jubilation died.

The thing that hung above him was stretched along the far wall of the cavern, pinned to the stone as though it were a flayed hide. From it dangled the filaments that glowed so delicately. The surface of the thing was pitted and scarred, striated along both side by gill slits. At its center was a face, a mouthless and hollow parody of a human skull. It leered at Krýl with empty sockets, the sharp lines of its sparse features terrible and gaunt.

Krýl reached up a hand, hesitated, let it drop. The fibers swayed, waving back and forth as he drew breath, then let it out, drew breath, then let it out.

When it moved Krýl told himself to run. To his surprise he could not. He tried to throw himself to the side and again found that he was rooted in place. As the filaments that hung overhead elongated, slithering down to brush at his face, Krýl could only whimper. A moment later and they were in his eyes, his nose, his mouth, his ears. He gagged and coughed, grabbed at the tendrils, tried to pull them free. They would not go, but only wound themselves deeper. With a jerk Krýl fell to one side amidst a shower of droplets. He did not feel his head strike stone, nor the water that closed over him.

He could smell moist air, rich earth, the sweetness of decay. It rose all around him, filled him, drew him in. He could feel the wet earth, smell the moldering leaves, taste the droplets of water that seeped into the soil. Then came the sun through the canopy. It shone on ranks of trees that rose like battlements, the air between them teeming with insects. Golden shafts of light broke through the boughs overhead, casting moving shadows on fallen logs and sprouting fungi. All was verdant, alive, teeming, thriving; an organism made up of a hundred thousand different species.

Krýl knew this memory was old, an echo from a past gone and buried. It came from a time before the continents had fractured, before the sun had grown swollen and red; before the seas had begun to burn away leaving nothing but desert in their wake.

Feeling the forest around him, the ebb and flow of life, death, and rebirth, Krýl forgot that he lay in a cave below a mountain's worth of granite and crystal. He watched, felt, and heard eons pass in the blink of an eye. He saw cataclysm, the rise and fall of mountains; life flourishing and abundant, then desolate and sparse. It went on and on, a diminishing cycle growing ever weaker. Finally, there was hunger.

Krýl jerked upright. Around him water sloshed, the blue glow from the pool fading, fading. In near darkness he began to feel his way out of the pool. He scratched at the lichen, dragged himself onto the bare rocks.

When he lifted his hand to clear the water from his eyes, Krýl stared in disbelief at the jagged gauntlet that covered his fingers and palm. He closed these fingers into a fist, opened them, closed them again. Then, lowering his hand, he looked down at his chest, his belly, his groin, his legs. Reaching up, he tentatively touched his face. Everywhere he was encased in the same armored carapace.

Then came the hunger.

It rose in him like a wave of sand on the back of a desert wind. It was the need of centuries spent underground, of countless ages of privation. It was all consuming, pushing aside every other thought, emotion, and impulse.

When the fungoid shell urged Krýl towards the unspoiled meat in the cavern above he did not resist. Getting to his feet he began to climb back the way he had come.

Six

As he walked, bits of crystal fell from the remains of his cloak, and the notched surface of the armor. With each step more pieces dropped to the broken ground leaving a minute trail. Uncaring, Krýl trudged through hills and scrubland, around boulder fields, along the rim of a crevasse like an open wound on the face of the earth. Slowly, steadily, he made his way back towards the caravan.

This had been his third caravan since the dry season

ended, since the winds had died and the storms should have abated. To have been caught in a squall so early in the year was an aberration. The toll it had taken on him, severe.

Rounding a low stone edifice he caught sight of the train of wagons, carts, outriders, and palanquins. Krýl's heart sank. He pushed the empty feeling in his chest aside along with the armor's continued insistence on being fed.

Down the slope he went, picking his was through brush and deadfall, the bundle in his arms seeming to put on weight with each step. When he reached the caravan Krýl scuffed to halt, trying his best to keep his legs from shaking. The man and woman who had been watching his approach regarded him with identical expressions. Krýl bent low and placed the bundle at their feet.

The man scratched at the week's worth of stubble on his chin, his lips pressed tight together. "Is this…?"

Krýl nodded at the bundle of rags.

The woman scoffed, crossed and uncrossed her arms.

"Where's the girl? We hired you to get the girl."

Krýl pointed. "This is how I found her."

"This?" asked the woman, jabbing a finger at the tiny thing on the ground.

"Yes."

The woman raised her head, eyes brimming. She nodded. The man put his head in his hands and sobbed. He knelt beside the bundle and began to tug at the bunch of rags.

"No," said Krýl. "Bury her as she is."

The man looked up at Krýl.

"Bury her as she is."

From further down the line of wagons a voice was raised. Krýl turned towards the speaker and saw a thin man in an embroidered robe raise his hand and wave. "Is that her?" His voice was high and expectant. "Is that the girl?"

At Krýl's feet, the man nodded. The woman crossed her arms again and hugged herself. "What's left of her."

The thin man drew to a halt and put a hand to his mouth. "Gods below, gods above…" He ran the hand over his narrow chin and tugged at his scruff of beard. "…have mercy."

The woman put a fingernail in her mouth and bit at it. "She won't be pleased…we were supposed to deliver the girl alive. She won't pay us now that she's dead."

The thin man bobbed his head up and down, up and down. "If we're fortunate we may be able to cross the border and remove ourselves from her territory before she catches wind of us. If we stay and she discovers that the child she bought is dead…"

Krýl looked down at the fellow huddled over the bundle of rags, at the woman, at the thin man. "What do you mean deliver her alive? Who won't pay you? You told me she was your daughter."

The woman scoffed. "We lied."

"We have to go," said the man still huddled over the bundle of rags. He began to weep.

Someone at the front of the caravan began to shout.

"No time," said the thin man. "Look."

A dozen yards ahead a man stood on the top of a wagon pointing off into the distance. Krýl followed the line of the man's gesture to a ridge a half a league away. Atop the rise stood a line of mounted figures, lances in hand. At the center of the line the silhouette of a woman sat atop an enormous hýthric.

Krýl shaded his eyes and looked again. No, the woman was not a silhouette. It was almost as if the morning light passed straight through her.

The thin man turned haunted eyes to Krýl. "Run."

COMES A WITCH

————•●•————

One

The thin man made for the relative cover of the scrub and boulders. Once he had reached the broken scattering of rocks his progress slowed. Krýl watched as he began to pick his way over the deadfall and between thorn bushes. Another dozen pace and the thin man tripped, went down. Getting back to his feet, he tugged his robe free of the clinging undergrowth and continued to clamber away from the wagons. Krýl shook his head and turned back towards the caravan.

To every side the caravaners scrambled to collect their belongings and turn their wagons. Dust rose from the hooves of the milling draft animals. The bedlam of this hurried attempt at flight created a snarl of vehicles that saw the caravan unable to move forward or back. Drovers shouted to one another in desperation, crying for the slower wagons to be pushed aside. Here and there women and children could be seen running amidst the flurry of animals and the billowing dust.

At Krýl's feet lay the bundle of rags. The child inside was so slight it seemed pointless for the wormrotters to have taken her. The man and woman he had mistook for the child's guardians huddled together a short way off, their bent backs half obscured by the waves of dust. The man continued to weep into his hands while the woman remained stolid, her face hard.

Turning to the distant hill on which had appeared the cause of all this tumult, Krýl saw the line of mounted warriors begin its descent towards the caravan.

Krýl felt the carapace twitch. The symbiotic armor had all but forgotten the bundle of rags, Krýl having brow-beaten it into silence. The eukaryotic shell no longer cared for the dead girl; it could smell the fear that rolled off the caravan in waves.

Within moments the riders were among the wagons.

With serpentine grace the line of cavalry wound in and around of the roiling tangle of wagons. With long, thin lances and pounding hooves they broke the cursory resistance the caravaners raised against them. When these clusters of guardsmen were scattered they turned their attention to riding down the merchants and journeymen. Screams rose from the jumbled mass of wagons as the riders thrust and cut, staining the dust of the road in a dozen different shades of red.

Krýl watched as a vintner was run through, dying amidst broken heaps of wine barrels. A moment later he saw a woman in a burqa of white and sewn with gold swept over a saddle, her legs thrashing.

Two guardsmen leapt from the back of a wagon onto one of the riders, pulling him down. They died on the lances of the next wave.

Krýl planted his feet, crossed his arms over his chest. He watched as the riders continued to dodge and weave amongst the wagons. He waited as the armor squirmed, rippled.

The first of the lancers to reach him came thundering across the broken ground at a hard gallop. Krýl stood his ground. The rider's lance was aimed at his chest, the point steady. Krýl let the blade come within a foot of his breastplate before stepping within the rider's guard. Reaching up with taloned hands he pulled the man from his saddle and drove him into the ground.

The rider hit the road with a sharp cry, his turban and pointed helmet tumbling from his head. Krýl drove his fist through the man's ribs, splitting armor, bone, and the soft tissue beneath. The rider died without another sound, his eyes wide.

Krýl raised his head and watched as the now-riderless hýthric trotted from the killing ground and into the field of boulders beyond. Its long neck bobbing up and down the animal looked about, seemingly nonplussed.

A wet sucking noise drew Krýl's attention from the wandering hýthric. He looked down.

Sprouting from the hand buried in the lancer's chest, the armor began to extend tendrils throughout the wound. Blood, siphoned from the heart and lungs, flowed through the tendrils and into the carapace. Krýl gritted his teeth and tried to concentrate upon something, anything, besides the sensation of the armor drinking the lancer dry. It did him little good. As the tendrils began to expand and move, excising bits of meat and shunting them into the symbiote, Krýl felt every ounce of flesh it absorbed.

The carapace blossomed. It flooded Krýl with a wealth of sensory information. He saw the well-choreographed movements of the lancers, how they herded and controlled the random flight of the caravaners. In his nostrils the coppery tang of blood mingled with the smell of dust, and sweat, and late blooming corpse flowers tucked into a far corner of the valley. There was another scent as well—something exotic, something new...

Before he had a chance to pinpoint this new scent, the tip of a lance cut the air mere inches from his face. Krýl balked, instinctively raising one hand and batting the weapon aside. The tip struck the hard-packed earth and stuck. The momentum of the rider bowed the shaft, over-extending the wood. As the lance shattered and splinters burst around him, Krýl pulled his fist from inside the dead man.

A split second later and the rider thundered past. Krýl deftly extended one hand and grasped the man's ankle, sweeping him from his saddle. He struck the ground with a grunt and the sound of breaking bones.

At first the rider did not scream. Then, as the shock of his fall abated, he began to bellow. His arms moved spasmodically, his hands grasping at nothing. Beneath him the lancer's shattered pelvis and back were twisted at an awkward angle, his legs unmoving.

Another tentacle burst from the armor. It scythed through the air, striking the broken soldier in the face. A moment later and it had reduced the man's features to little more than scored bone.

As greater and greater quantities of protein, calcium, fats, and amino acids were siphoned from the fallen lancer, Krýl felt the armor expand. The more it ate, the greater its desire. By the time it had fully exsanguinated the first of the dead men, the semi-sentient thing was nearly beyond the point of being controlled. Having gone so long without feeding it was like a starved aýrs-hound, its needs nearly overriding Krýl's urging towards caution. He fought to keep it in check.

A dozen lances, their tips gleaming in the sunlight, leveled themselves at Krýl. He saw them as if from a distance, his perception of the objects detached from their intended purpose. On a conscious level he knew they were meant for him, knew that they would be driven through the armor and into his flesh. Somehow he could not connect this thought with the sight of the sun heliographing from their polished edges. He saw them come closer, then closer. In the space of a few heartbeats they would be on him. He would die while only half-conscious of his surroundings, run down like an animal.

"Hold."

The word was spoken softly, yet seemed to fill the turbulent air. It penetrated the thunder of hooves and the screams of the dying. The single syllable, clear and feminine, seemed to quell the torrent of violence.

As one, the riders drew on their reins, grinding their mounts to a halt. The wave of dust raised by the hýthric washed over Krýl, momentarily blinding him. When it had cleared, he saw that the riders were sitting as still as statues.

Krýl fought against the chemical stew filling his brain. He beat at the fungoid interloper that wriggled in his mind and forced it, inch by agonizing inch, to cease its thrashing. Slowly, ever so slowly, consciousness began to return.

Krýl cursed himself, struck his bloodied fist on his thigh. He had nearly allowed the armor free reign. This had almost cost him his life. Again he shoved at the intruding fibrils at the back of his mind. At last the armor retreated.

For what seemed an eternity, Krýl stood hunched beside the two dead lancers. Despite being forced from his brain the armor continued to feed. To have attempted to refuse it would have been impossible. Krýl could keep it from killing more men, but not from finishing what lay before it.

Krýl watched the faces of the lancers on their hýthric as the armor gorged itself; he saw their disgust, saw their fear as well. None wished to be the first to approach. Be that as it may, Krýl was certain that all would have gladly run him through.

The line of soldiers broke then. The men shuffling their hýthric to the side creating an aisle wide enough for a single rider. That rider made its way towards the front ranks and halted just outside the line of soldiers. Krýl regarded the figure, unmoving save for the twitch of the feeding tendrils. The rider regarded him in turn.

"You," said the same strong, feminine voice that had filled his head a moment ago. Krýl shivered involuntarily.

"I have never seen your like before."

Krýl did not respond, could not respond. The sensation of words floating not only through the air, but also through his mind, had sealed his lips.

Reaching to the hood that covered her face the rider drew it back to reveal a cascade of hair that was a green so bright it seemed to fluoresce.

Krýl inhaled sharply.

The rider laughed. "I'd wager you've never seen my like before either. It would seem we have much to speak of, you and I. Let us call a truce so that we may speak with one another like civilized beings."

She smiled then and the chill Krýl felt redoubled.

Two

"Tell me, are you a man in the guise of a beast, or a beast that thinks it is a man?"

Her lips were full and green, the teeth behind them

straight and white. Krýl watched them move, heard the words they spoke aloud and in the back of his mind.

"Surely you can speak. I can see in your eyes there's more to you than mere animus."

The woman's features were severe, handsome, even regal. Her cheekbones were high, the line of her jaw straight. But for Krýl, the woman's beauty was offset by her bizarrely translucent skin. It drew his attention from her features, transfixed him, made him gape like a simpleton. Beneath her skin the woman's musculature was just as vitreous, crossed by a network of blood vessels that lent her whole appearance a spectral quality.

Not for the first time Krýl was glad of his armored face-plate. The strain that would otherwise have shown on his face would have earned him either contempt or a grave.

"Don't be shy," said the woman, "speak up. Tell me your name." She blinked once, slowly, deliberately.

Krýl yanked at one of the tendrils still rooting around the chest cavity of the man at his feet. The armor thrashed, tried to reconnect the tendril. Krýl retracted the nascent append-age, then set to work retrieving the others. Slowly, with much effort, he pulled another fibril back within the carapace, then another.

The woman before him watched as the tendrils disap-peared one by one. "Your name, if you please."

Krýl looked to the lucent woman, then to her lancers. The men still sat upon their mounts, lances couched, tips pointed at his heart.

"Very well," said the woman, drawing up her robes and slipping from her saddle.

As her feet touched the cracked and bloodied earth the lancers stirred. One of them reached for her saying, "Mis-tress, do not." She silenced him with a wave of her hand.

Stepping gingerly over the heaped bodies she made her way towards Krýl. The wind stirred, fluttering robes, lifting them so they seemed to float around her.

The woman took several more steps then halted. Krýl wrenched free another tendril.

"Your name?"

More wind, more fluttering robes. Krýl tugged, retrieved the last of the tendrils.

The woman raised her chin. "I am known by many as the Pellucid Witch. Those who serve me simply call me Mistress."

Krýl turned his head to one side, concentrated on asserting his will over the carapace. Slowly the armor's protests at being separated from its meal began to wane. It turned inward, processing the flesh it had already gathered.

The Pellucid Witch tucked a lock of hair back over her ear and narrowed her eyes. "I know there are thoughts behind your eyes; I can see them, but I cannot hear them. My raiders, the people of this caravan, even the animals… their minds are all open to me. You, on the other hand, are like a tome scrawled in a hand I can only half decipher. You can hear me, the thoughts and commands I project, even from a distance. I can see that as well. On the other hand, I am left almost deaf to your thoughts. Why is this?"

Krýl shook his head. "Couldn't say."

A smile tugged at the corners of the Witch's lips. "So you can speak. Tell me, do you think it is the armor? Does that shell keep me from entering your mind?"

Krýl shrugged.

The Witch raised one hand to her mouth and bit at the tip of her thumbnail. The hint of a smile she wore broke into a coquettish little grin. She gazed up at Krýl through lashes that were as green as her hair. "I adore things that are new and strange, things that are unusual even for a world as bizarre as this one."

Krýl regarded the Witch. The membranes that covered his eyes sharpened the outline of her face, the men behind her, the lances they still held at the ready. Krýl tried to make sense of what he had seen flicker behind the Witch's eyes. He thought it was more than simple curiosity. To him that momentary gleam looked covetous.

The armor opened vents along Krýl's cheeks, drew breath, tasted the air.

The Witch's eyes widened. "Marvelous…"

Krýl shook out the tension in his shoulders, his arms. "What can I do for you?"

The Witch dropped her hand to her throat, playful grin still on her lips. "I want you to be my guest."

"Your guest?"

"Yes. Your employment as a caravan guard is at an end, that much is obvious. Now that you are no longer under contract why not take my silver? I will pay far better than these merchants and drovers."

Krýl let his gaze stray from the Witch's face. He scanned the jumble of wagons, the spilled cargo, the bodies lying in the dust. The wreckage of the caravan extended for nearly a hundred yards in either direction. The guardians of the child he had retrieved remained huddled next to their wagon. Before them the remains of the girl lay wrapped in Krýl's cloak. At the sight of her he felt his stomach knot. Turning back to the Witch he said simply, "No."

The Witch's face fell. "And why not?" She swept a hand towards the wreck of the caravan. "Have you so much to lose? Look at them. These cowards were unable to defend themselves or their property. Their weakness has lost them their livelihoods. I offer you a chance to earn ten times what you would have been paid by this rabble. Why refuse me?"

Krýl ignored the Witch and instead pointed at the bundle of rags. "I walked a day, and a night, and a day to bring that girl back from the men who took her. What of her?"

The Witch followed his gesture. "What indeed? I purchased her months ago. She was to be brought to me, alive and well fed. I hired these fools to see to it that my purchase was cared for. They have failed."

"What need do have you of a child?"

"As I have said," replied the Witch, "I am a collector of strange and interesting things. This child was special. She would have made a fine addition to my menagerie. Now corpse flowers will grow from her grave. She is of no value to me."

"Why bother with all...this?" Krýl swept a hand towards the ruined caravan. "Why spill blood when you've already paid?"

The green-haired woman first sneered then laughed. "Sport. My own amusement. Profit. Why take just the child when I could have the whole caravan?"

The interlocking plates that covered his face first split, then drew back. Krýl stood looking down into the Witch's face. Her eyes were dark, the pupil and iris almost indistinguishable. "Show me your silver," he said.

The Witch gestured to her lancers and the tips of their lances were raised. One of the men put a hand inside his tunic and came up with a pouch. He tossed it to Krýl who caught it without taking his eyes from the Witch. He weighed the contents in his palm, then poked one taloned finger into the opening at its top. Inside, the tiny ingots gleamed.

"You see?" cooed the Witch. Again Krýl felt his chest contract. If it was some latent moral compunction it would have to remain unexpressed. Taking money from butchers was nothing new. He was a mercenary, and if he was to live he would have to earn.

Krýl nodded. "As you said."

The Pellucid Witch beamed up at him. "You may call me Mistress."

Turning on her heel, she strode back to her mount, her hips swaying beneath the thin folds of her robe. She waved off the hand one of her lancers offered and climbed nimbly back into her side saddle.

After a moment Krýl followed, gripping the bag of silver tight in one armored fist.

Three

"Another day at the most, then we'll see the end of the scrubland. After that it's half a day's ride to the keep."

Krýl nodded. The Witch smiled. Beneath him the hýthric he had been lent plodded steadily forward. Overhead the sun beat down from a sky that shone like bloodied copper. There were no clouds, only an ashen haze that clung to the edge of the horizon.

A branch scraped at Krýl's carapaced shoulder, its leaves clattering like dry bones. Krýl prodded his hýthric to the right, away from the offending limb. The animal grunted. Another tree reached for him and he swatted it away. Its bark was white, its leaves a deep green. They grew from the top of a bulbous trunk that tapered towards the tangle of branches that sprouted from its peak. At its base was a mass of roots that clung uncertainly to the anemic soil.

In every direction the landscape was dotted with the pale, stunted trees. They grew in evenly spaced clusters, their branches nearly overlapping. None of the hýthric stopped to much at them. Krýl said as munch.

"They know the leaves are poisonous. The sap as well. The trees are useless to the animals, but we cultivate them anyway. When boiled and fermented the sap makes a liquor that is at once sweet and bitter. I will give you a bottle if you like."

Krýl nodded. "Kind of you."

The Witch adjusted her hood and returned to watching the trail ahead. Behind them the column of lancers and captured wagons rumbled on.

There was little conversation, even amongst the cavalrymen. Krýl marveled at the level of discipline the men displayed. They were unlike any unit he had ever marched with. The free companies that had employed him in days past would have been alive with drinking, boasting, the occasional brawl. The Witch's lancers, by contrast, rode in two perfect columns, lances at their sides.

Over the trudge of hooves and the clatter of wheels the sound of weeping drifted up the column towards Krýl. He glanced behind, but could not see who was doing the whimpering.

"Does that mewling offend you?"

Krýl glanced at the Witch. "No."

"If it does I will have the one responsible beaten. Or flayed. Simply say so and it will be done."

"I'm not offended."

"Very well."

For a time they rode in silence. More of the bulbous trees passed languidly by. Amongst their roots skittered small lizards. They clung to the smooth bark, dark eyes alert. They watched as Krýl and the column passed, darting for cover when a shadow fell across their backs.

"Perhaps I will have them beaten anyway," The Witch glanced back over her shoulder. "It will show the rest of the slaves what is expected of them. Strict discipline from the outset. To allow such behavior to go unchecked shows a lack of conviction. Slaves will take advantage of such a lapse and will foment rebellion."

"It's only weeping."

Another sob drifted up from one of the caravaneer's pilfered wagons. The vehicle had been converted to a cage, a rolling prison for those unfortunate enough to have lived through the massacre.

The Witch raised her hand. This gesture was echoed by one of the lancers and passed down the line. The double file of men and hýthric ground to a halt. Turning in her saddle the Witch said, "Fetch me the wailer."

The nearest lancer nodded and rode back along the column. Krýl waited, listening to the sounds of a cage being unlocked. Then the rider returned with a figure slung across his saddle. Krýl recognized the man whom he had taken to be the father of the dead girl. When the Witch caught sight of him she pursed her lips.

The lancer drew rein, took the man by the hair, and lifted his head.

The Witch leaned in close and narrowed her eyes. "You have disturbed my guest."

From where he was slung over the lancer's saddle the man raised his head as best he could. Tears stained his flabby cheeks, cutting rivulets through the grime caked on his face. His hair was a rat's nest, his clothes filthy. Even at a distance of six feet or more, Krýl could smell the man.

"Is it for the child that you weep?" asked the Witch. "Or do you lament your own fate?"

The man lowered his eyes, fresh tears falling to the sandy ground.

Raising an eyebrow the Witch said, "As I have said, your

blubbering has disturbed my guest. This I cannot abide."

Another sob tried to escape the man. He held it at bay as best he could, his body hitching. The Witch sneered.

"Throw him off."

The lancer dumped the man from his saddle. He hit the ground with a puff of dust and an agonized grunt.

Krýl glanced at the Witch. "This isn't necessary."

The Witch waved his words away. "Nonsense. You are a guest in my lands and therefore your comfort is paramount. If you are disturbed in the slightest then the situation must be remedied."

Swinging one leg over her hýthric the Witch dropped lightly to the ground. The lancer that had retrieved the sobbing man followed suit. Amidst the swirling film of her robes the Witch strode to the huddled lump that languished in the dust. In her wake came the lancer, his features implacable.

The Witch knelt before the prostrate man and lifted his chin with one finger. "I paid you quite a lot of money to steal that girl and bring her to me. You in turn allowed her to be taken from you. If it wasn't for my guest, not even her body would have been recovered. I would have had to spend the rest of my days wondering what had become of my purchase. Now, to add insult to injury, you offend my guest. You disturb what was otherwise a peaceful ride through the countryside."

Krýl shifted uneasily in his saddle. "I'm not offended. I was merely curious."

The Witch sighed theatrically. "Do you see how polite he is? Even in light of your grievous offenses he still acts the gentleman."

The man lowered his forehead to the ground. He clawed at the sand with pudgy fingers, clenching and unclenching his fists. He said something under his breath, something Krýl could not hear.

"What was that?" asked the Witch.

"I'm sorry," said the man. "I'm sorry!"

"That is simply not enough."

The Witch gestured to the lancer who drew his knife and stepped forward.

Krýl turned away as the lancer wedged the blade sideways into the man's mouth. When he was done and the weeping man's thrashing had abated the lancer threw something aside. The armor twitched, urging Krýl to go after the bit of flesh. He ignored it.

"Put him with the others," said the Witch, rising.

Krýl watched as the man was dragged back towards to the cage by two of the lancers, his feet trailing in the dust, blood streaming down his chin.

"Unnecessary," said Krýl.

The Witch shrugged. "Perhaps. But he cost me the girl. I would say he owes me far more than what I have taken." She then mounted, sliding effortlessly into the side-saddle that topped her hýthric. "I hope that did not put you off your dinner. Tonight we shall roast the birds Kaalah shot at the last river crossing."

Krýl turned to the lancer that had done the knife work on the weeping man. He in turn fixed Krýl with a dark-eyed stare, his gaze as utterly devoid of emotion as that of the Witch. Krýl held the man's eyes for a moment, waited until the other looked away.

From the direction of the wagons a woman screamed.

"Come," said the Witch. "We have several hours of riding ahead of us before we must stop for the night. The going will be easier now and soon enough we will be home."

Four

More than a dozen warlords claiming to be a Prince of the Blood, rightful heir to this land or that, had bought Krýl's sword. He had seen the shabby little keeps they called palaces. He had stormed several of the same, toppling the lordlings who had allowed his contract to expire. Killing them had not been for the sake of vengeance or malice it was simply the job. Regardless, Krýl's disdain for the war-lords' claims had galled him. Their dissimulation made him ill. By contrast, the fortress the Pellucid Witch laid claim to was like none of the others he had seen or taken. Should Krýl live a thousand years, it was unlikely he would ever see its equal.

The fortress sat atop a natural promontory that dominated the rolling plain below. Built of red stone, the walls seemed to grow from the living rock. Bits of crystal set within the stones sparkled in the glow of the low hanging sun. The cast of the dying light made the walls appear to burn, their sheer sides alive with alternating hues of carmine and vermilion. To look upon those high battlements Krýl was forced to shade his eyes as the column made its approach.

Built around the base of the promontory was another wall, the defensive curtain made of the same reddish stone as the keep. Between this secondary fortification and the fortress above could be seen trees, shrubbery, succulents of a thousand different varieties. These clusters of herbage were crisscrossed by paths paved with the same stones that comprised the walls, red against red.

Atop his hýthric, Krýl sat and gaped.

The Witch glanced at him out of the corner of one eye. "They are beautiful, are they not? These gardens of mine have been cultivated over decades, the plants imported from every corner of the world."

Krýl looked to the Witch, then back to the expanse of green.

In the south even the richest of men could hardly boast more than a few withered trees in clay pots. Here, at the edge of the known world, was a woman with gardens the sight of which would have dropped most nobles to their knees.

The Witch looked from the distant gardens to the line of passing lancers. The path the soldiers trod led to a gate topped by a barbican and twin turrets. Slowly, the double column passed from the light and into the shadows beneath the fortifications.

"Do you see?" asked the Witch, pointing. "In the east, beyond the mountains?"

Krýl raised a hand, shading his eyes from the glare reflecting off the keep. He scanned the distant ridgeline. Above it could be seen tendrils of airborne crystal. They reached greedily towards the sky. Below them was only darkness.

"The storm will reach the mountains soon," said the Witch, "but there it will remain. This place sits in a basin surrounded on three sides by mountains." Turning, she pointed to the north and to the west. "It is these mountains that keep the storms at bay. Because of them I am able to cultivate my gardens in the open."

Krýl grunted. He had seen very few places which had escaped the brunt of the storms. In most, the crystals had stripped the landscape, scored the very rocks. Here, in this valley, the Witch had found a veritable paradise.

In the west the sun slipped further towards the mountains. Overhead a gossamer layer of clouds began to burn.

The Witch's lips spread in a grin. "Is it not grand? In all the world this place is unique. Nowhere else will you find a greater collection of plant and animal life. The treasures contained within my keep are priceless beyond measure. I hold wealth that the warlords of the south can only dream of."

Krýl did not know what to say. He simply sat and watched as the last of the wagons trundled through the gate.

"Come," said the Witch. "Come and see what I have made."

Five

Krýl could not name a single one of the flowers, the trees, the succulents, the hedges. Each bore foliage that was striking in its own right, but utterly foreign to him. His eyes flitted from one growth to the next. Never had he imagined there were so many colors or scents, so many different types of birds and insects.

For its part, the eukaryotic shell opened the vents along Krýl's torso, breathing in as deeply as he. Small tendrils flitted from his wrists, ankles, and shoulders grasping at branches and snatching at the insects that wandered by. It took an effort to restrain the carapace, to keep it from sampling everything in sight.

Beside him the Witch paced slowly. Her hands were clasped behind her back, her robes adrift on the breeze.

"There is a well beneath the keep. It is fed by an aquifer that flows from out of the bedrock. Years ago I tapped it and had an irrigation system of my own design buried just below the surface of the garden. Water flows from the aquifer into these pipes and thence into the garden. Because of this it blooms year round."

Krýl lifted his hand to brush at an overhanging branch, then withdrew it again. "I've never seen a place like this."

The Witch smiled. "Very few have, or ever will."

Krýl turned back to the trees, the flowers. He did not

dare reach out and touch them lest the armor's greed get the better of him. To clip a bud, purposefully or otherwise, might be an invitation to disaster.

"Now this," said the Witch, "is something unique even amongst my many treasures." She drew to a halt and raised her head. Krýl followed her gaze.

It was tall and slender, curved like a cluster of vines. At a height just above the level of a man's head, the plant swelled outwards. From the top of the tangle of vines grew a pale green bulge that seemed to pulse in a slow rhythm. On its underside were ridged layers of what appeared to be rubbery, yellowish skin. Its top was mottled with crimson spots and dripping with a thick, viscous sap. At the sight of the thing Krýl wrinkled his nose.

The Witch laughed.

"It does have a rather...unique appearance. This has not escaped my notice."

"You said it, not me."

The Witch laughed again. "You needn't have worried. I bred it that way—not for beauty, but for function. Its design was my own. After much research I chose the form I thought most efficient."

"Efficient?"

"Yes," said the Witch, "efficiency is paramount. You've plied the wastes; you know that only those plants and animals that are efficient at hunting, at finding water, at conserving energy survive. The same can be said of my creation."

"And what is it so efficient at, this creation of—"

The scream came from the direction of the keep. It rebounded off the secondary curtain, then died amongst the trees. Krýl turned sharply towards the fortress.

Though the garden was in shadow the upper battlements remained drenched in the last of the dying light. From their height dangled a single figure. It was hung from a chain, loops of intestines spilling from its open belly. It swung to and fro, viscera staining the already crimson stones.

"Well, that's an end to all that unpleasantness with the girl." The Witch looked up at the wall and sighed. "Perhaps his remains will serve as a reminder to others that I do not tolerate failure. When I have grown tired of looking at him I will use his corpse to fertilize my garden." She lowered her head and smiled. "Despite the death of the child, this venture was not a complete loss. I discovered you, didn't I?"

Krýl turned slowly from the butchered man hanging from the battlements. When his gaze fell on the Witch he saw that she had already parted her robes, the diaphanous fabric puddling about her ankles. When she caught his eye, she opened her hands and let the rest of the garment fall.

She was sublime. Nearly any man would have killed for a moment with her. Despite the horror dangling over-head, Krýl knew he was no exception.

Beneath the Witch's translucent flesh flowed the same intricate network of blood vessels that highlighted her cheeks. They followed the curve of her breasts, her belly, extending down her torso to join with the network that threaded its way over the limpid musculature beneath. Krýl followed their progress, pausing at the patch of hair at her loins as green as that upon her head.

The Witch raised one thumb to her mouth and bit delicately at the nail. "What lies beneath all that armor?"

Krýl cleared his throat. "Just a man. Nothing more, nothing less."

"Hmm." The Witch stepped closer. She lifted her hands and placed them on his shoulders. Krýl drew back. She raised an eyebrow. "Are you afraid of me? Afraid I may try to bite?"

"No," said Krýl. "The armor, it's—"

"It does not concern me," said the Witch. "Trees, flowers, succulents, fungi…all manner of growing things bow to my will. Your armor will not harm me."

Gently she laid her hands on his shoulders. Krýl winced and again tried to pull away. The Witch held firm. A heartbeat later he felt the carapace withdraw from the place where the Witch had touched it. Krýl's eyes went wide.

Slowly the Witch drew her hands down his chest. In their wake the eukaryotic shell retreated, peeling back one ragged layer after another. On his skin he felt gentle fingers, the rush of the breeze. Gooseflesh rose along his chest, his belly. The Witch bit her lip. Reaching up to the back of his neck she drew him down to the grass.

Krýl did not protest.

THE MENAGERIE

One

The moon was high, its glow painting the gardens below in shades of silver and gray. Amongst the herbage, alternating patches of light and shadow stood out in stark relief. From Krýl's vantage the groves of succulents, copses of broad-leafed trees, and winding beds of flowers looked as though they had been carved out of stone.

In the distance a night bird called, was answered, called again. Krýl squinted into the shadows, peering at the spaces the moon did not touch. He could see nothing but grass and leaves. Still Krýl looked, and Krýl listened.

The sound came again, muffled and barely audible. Krýl looked from one section of the garden to another. There was no sign of movement. He held his breath, strained his ears, concentrated on the sigh of the wind and the chirp of insects. His efforts went unrewarded.

Again, Krýl looked, and Krýl listened. As the minutes passed he became less and less sure he had heard anything at all. Nevertheless, he remained. To brush aside a noise, no matter how slight, could be the death of a soldier.

Krýl raised his eyes to the moon. It had moved, perhaps two degrees past its zenith. That meant another three hours before dawn. He scratched at his temple. Those hours could be spent in dreamless sleep; sleep without the eukaryotic shell chattering away at the back of his brain. He would not have to pace aimlessly while it scented the wind, urging him to hunt, and hunt, and hunt.

At the Witch's touch the shell had receded, drawn back into itself. Its constant prodding had first waned, then faded. When the Witch had drawn her fingers down his chest Krýl had felt as though his heart might burst. When she had beckoned, he had followed.

A rustle of silk and the pad of bare feet on stone made him turn. Krýl watched as the Pellucid Witch stepped from the shadows and onto the moonlit balcony. She glided to the railing, drew up beside him. He regarded her for a long moment, then turned back to the gardens.

Leaning her cheek on his shoulder the Witch raised one hand and touched his bicep. He could feel the heat of her skin, her warmth a counterpoint to the night air.

"They are beautiful in the moonlight, my gardens." The Witch's voice was as soft as the silks she wore. "All their color is washed away and they repose in perfect, achromatic unity. There is nothing to distinguish the plants, one from the other, save their outline. The shape of each can be viewed independently—form and depth, line and texture."

For a time Krýl did not speak. He stood regarding the woman beside him, watching as the moonlight was caught and refracted by her nearly translucent flesh. It played across the blood vessels that wound beneath her skin. To his eyes she appeared to be another exotic plant from the gardens below, a rare herb that could speak and reason.

"You seemed so peaceful," said the Witch, "so deep in the arms of Somnus. Why awaken now? Why come out here to stand with your face lined with worry?"

"A sound."

"A sound?"

"From the gardens."

The Witch raised one eyebrow. "You don't say?"

"I do."

"Strange," said the Witch, "I have never known the plants to speak before."

Krýl turned from her to look out over the gardens.

"Not even the hint of a smile," said the Witch. "What a pity. And here I thought I was being so ghastly clever. It appears that my wit is not what I thought it to be." She somehow managed to pout and smile at the same time.

Krýl glanced at her out of the corner of one eye. "The joke wasn't lost on me."

The exaggerated pout continued, was joined by crinkled brows. "Poor fellow. Has it really been so long since you've had a reason to laugh?"

Krýl thought for a moment, shrugged.

"What a shame," said the Witch. "Still, I won't press the issue. We shall work our way up from a simple smile and see where that leads."

So saying she pressed herself closer, one hand straying from his arm and down his belly. Krýl felt her breast against his arm, her breath on his shoulder.

"Come back to bed," said the Witch. "I will tease that smile from you. Just wait and see if I don't."

Krýl went, allowing her to lead him back through the pillared arches that opened onto her chamber. He fell with her into the pile of cushions, silks, and furs that served as her bed. When the sound from the garden came again he paid it no mind.

Two

"There are a great many things I wish to show you, but I fear some may be of interest only to me."

The Witch looked down at the stones of the path then back up at the vista beyond the walls. Low on the eastern horizon clouds of crystalline shards caught and refracted the morning sun.

Krýl, his arm linked through hers, looked down at the Witch. Beside him the same light that shone on the distant storm glinted from the hood of her robe. The garment was simple, form-fitting, running the length of her frame with slits up the sides from ankles to hips. Its surface was metallic, flowing like liquid silver. As the Witch made her way down the flagstone path the movements of her muscles below the layers of cloth was hypnotic. Krýl found it difficult to look at anything else.

"I'd be glad to see whatever you want to show me."

The Witch turned her face up to Krýl and smiled. "At any given moment you know exactly the right thing to say. How is it that you've came by such manners?"

Krýl shook his head. "I haven't got manners. It's just my good fortune that I usually don't feel much like speaking. When I do I try to say as little as possible."

The Witch patted him on the arm. "Well said."

Beneath their feet the red flagstones were cool despite the rising temperature. In the underbrush small animals darted into view, then back under cover. They had long ears, pert little puffballs for tails. Krýl watched as a pair of them chased one another back and forth before again disappearing from view. When he raised his eyes he caught a glimpse of one of the strange trees the Witch had shown him the day before. The sickly yellow-green of its under-belly was visible behind a stand of angular succulents. He turned away, not wanting it to mar his view.

A grove of rubbery Caryophyllales that stood as tall as a man hove into view and Krýl drew up short. He blinked up at the cluster of carnivorous plants, hardly able to keep his surprise in check. Languidly the massive structures flexed their serrated lobes, opening and closing them as though they were gaping mouths. Krýl could clearly see their pink insides, the sticky surfaces bristling with thousands of sensory fibrils.

The Witch spoke before Krýl could voice his question. "What manner of creatures do such plants seek to entrap? For so large a plant surely mere insects will not suffice."

Krýl nodded, sucked at one tooth.

"The short answer is that they eat whatever they can. The long answer involves my enemies, their ignominious defeat, and quite a lot of begging."

Krýl shook his head. "Amazing."

The Witch giggled. "Tell me—this technique of yours, has it served you well?"

"Hmm?" Krýl tried to pull his attention from the Caryophyllales, was partially successful.

"Holding your tongue. Speaking only when spoken to… has it served you well?"

"Thus far." Krýl took his attention from the grove of carnivorous plants and gave the Witch a half smile. He could feel sweat beginning to bead on his scalp and trickle down the back of his neck.

The Witch nudged him in the side. "That was not a full smile, but it will do for now."

The air had grown hot, the light more intense. At this altitude the sun felt somehow different, less filtered. With the eukaryotic shell hiding in patches along his neck and spine, Krýl felt it acutely.

"We have several hours before noon," said the Witch. "Shall we continue to walk the gardens, or would you prefer to see my collection of stolen art? Over the years I've amassed one of the finest galleries the world has ever seen. Some of the sculptures are relatively new, but most are as old as the mountains. The ancients made grand works of stone, metal, and ceramics. The shapes do not always make sense, but the quality of the materials and the craftsmanship is unparalleled."

Krýl opened his mouth to respond, but before he could the Witch went on.

"I've other collections as well, not just pretty things to look at. There is a hall of weapons and torture devices—indescribably cruel objects, some of which go back millennia. Or, perhaps, you would like to see the menagerie?"

Krýl shrugged.

The Witch sighed. "Even though your thoughts remain closed to me I can tell that something is bothering you. Tell me, what can I do to make your stay in my home more pleasurable?"

"It's nothing."

The Witch stopped and turned towards Krýl.

"You and I both know that when someone says It's nothing, that most certainly means it is something. Tell me."

Krýl waited a moment before answering. "The girl."

"The girl? The one you retrieved?"

Krýl nodded.

"Poor thing."

"She didn't die well."

"Not everyone does."

Krýl shook his head. "No, not everyone does."

The Witch turned towards the distant storm, watched the crystals chip away at the mountains.

"Perhaps you would like to see where she would have been kept, how she would have lived her life? It's more than a girl born to her circumstances could have ever hoped for."

Krýl stiffened. Feeling him go rigid the face of the Witch opened. "Ah, I see. You want to know what someone like me would want with a girl like her. Why purchase such a delicate flower? Why purchase another human being at all? She must be truly exceptional to warrant ferrying across the desert under armed guard."

The thought of the ragged little bundle he had carried drew Krýl's lips into a thin line. He had had to fight the armor through the entirety of the trek, forcing it to keep from sinking its tendrils into the tiny corpse and siphoning off whatever nutrients it found there.

At the back of his mind the fungoid shell began to buzz. It prodded Krýl, urging him to let it spread and envelope him. He shrugged it off, kept it sequestered.

"Does it speak to you?"

Krýl turned sharply towards the Witch. "How—"

The Witch rolled her eyes. "Your thoughts remain closed to me, I have already said as much. But I am a keen observer. I can see the gears turning in your mind. Until you feel the need to share your thoughts with me I shall simply have to guess at them. Fortunately for me, I am very good at reading people."

Krýl went back to pacing down the garden path.

For a time the two walked on in silence while around

them buzzed insects of every size, and shape, and color. In ever-changing motes they moved above the trees and flower beds, their shells reflecting the sunlight. To Krýl they looked like a living approximation of the crystalline storm raging to the east.

Drawing to a halt before a growth of succulents, their swollen fronds fanning outwards from a central bloom the color of dawn clouds, Krýl turned to the Witch.

"It does not speak, but it covets. What it wants it urges me to provide. Without my legs, my hands, my eyes, there's very little it can do to satisfy its hunger. It requires that I gather its food, or chase it down. When I feed it the thing rewards me."

The eyes of the Witch went very wide and her nails pressed into his arm. Krýl winced.

"It's a symbiote! I thought as much. By the look of it this armor of yours is a type of fungus. But if it is a eukaryote then how does it move on its own? Obviously the shell is a heterotroph, but I've never seen its like before. Tell me, is it strictly carnivorous? What it did to my men suggests as much, though I would not be surprised if it is an omnivore."

Under the barrage of questions Krýl stood dumbly, staring down at the Witch. He did not know whether to answer or allow his hostess to simply ramble on. She was the gardener, not he. The realm of plants was her domain; his was blood, and steel, and sand.

The Witch laughed and patted Krýl on the arm. "Just listen to me, going on as if I were a girl begging her tutor to tell her the secrets of the stars. Sadly, I know you do not have the answers I'm looking for. You have had to live with the thing, but its taxonomy could hardly have been your major concern."

Krýl allowed himself a wan smile. The Witch laughed

and pulled him closer. He relaxed slightly and allowed himself to enjoy the sound of her laughter and the feel of her arm wrapped in his.

Despite the chemical rewards the armor provided it denied him the touch of another human being. Whatever power the Witch possessed that had forced the shell to pull back—to leave him to his own devices for the first time in years—he thought it miraculous.

"Come," said the Witch, "I will show you the hall of weapons. You are a man who lives by the sword; as such, I am sure you will find many things of interest there. In return perhaps you could expand on what you have said regarding the armor? What sort of rewards does it provide? Chemical, I would imagine?"

She tugged at his arm, leading him towards the keep. Krýl moved with her for a few steps then stopped. "I want to see the menagerie."

The Witch looked at him for a moment, then with a smile she said, "Had enough of swords for the time being? Very well, we shall see the menagerie."

Three

At first glance it did not appear to have a beginning or an end. Krýl watched it coil around itself, an infinity of scales and barbed ridges. In the light that filtered through the overhead panes of glass, its back and sides shone a dull red ochre. It was a wurm, of that Krýl was certain, but the size of it was beyond anything he had seen before.

The Witch stood beside him, watching as Krýl examined the creature. Enrapt, he pressed himself against the thick wall of glass that separated the wurm's enclosure from the surrounding cages. As he bent closer the coils moved more rapidly, as if sensing his scrutiny.

"How long is it?"

"How long?" The Witch paused. "I've never actually measured the thing. It's impossible to get it to stretch out full length. I would approximate its length at over twenty feet."

Krýl's eyebrows lifted. The Witch raised one hand, her lips curled in a half smile. "I speak only truth."

Krýl turned towards the enclosure, then threw himself backwards. He landed on his backside, the fungoid armor writhing along the small of his back. The wurm stared sightlessly out at him, a mass of writhing armored coils. Krýl grimaced.

What passed for the wurm's face was split into four lobes that had been peeled back like the petals of a flower. Each was covered with hundreds of toothed spurs. At the center of this flower was a secondary mouth that slid obscenely in and out of the creature's throat. As its coils slid over and around each other, its neck weaving back and forth, the wurm's head remained perfectly still. It had fixated on Krýl, equally as enrapt as he had been.

The Witch chuckled to herself.

"You knew it would do that," said Krýl, getting to his feet, his face flush.

"Of course I did," smiled the Witch.

Krýl sniffed. Before him the wurm continued to sway, its proboscis sliding slowly forward and back, in and out of its throat.

"Come," said the Witch, "we should move on before it becomes agitated. The glass is four inches thick, but wurms are renowned for their ability to slither out of whatever cage confines them."

With a backwards glance at the scaled horror, Krýl followed as the Witch led him towards an arched doorway set at the opposite side of the menagerie.

As they walked they passed more enclosures, some of glass, others of intricately wrought iron bars. In a few of these cells languished creatures with which Krýl was already acquainted; great sand lizards, their hides the color of the desert floor, and giant rats with dull black eyes stared back at him, unblinking. Others were inhabited by unfamiliar things: bears the color of clouds, or moss-covered mammals that hung suspended by three clawed toes. Aeries containing dozens of species of birds rose three stories overhead, their occupants squawking and squalling. Several of the enclosures appeared to be empty until Krýl stopped and peered within. Upon closer inspection he saw they contained camouflaged tree snakes, or color-changing salamanders. In one of these glass enclosures seven brightly colored frogs sat upon the leaves of a flowering plant as exotic as any in the Witch's garden. Their skin was blue, their backs yellow with black spots. Krýl tapped the glass.

"I wouldn't advise that," said the Witch. "The touch of their skin is lethal. Besides, the tapping disturbs them."

Krýl snatched his hand away.

"When necessary I have my soldiers coat their daggers in the secretions from their backs. One nick with such a weapon and my enemies die choking and gasping for air. The toxin stills the diaphragm and the victim suffocates."

Krýl raised an eyebrow. The Witch smiled down at him. Straightening, he moved away from the glass case and its brightly colored frogs.

At the far end of the menagerie, beside a low archway, stood a lattice of iron bars. Behind the filigreed partition skittered a tribe of primates. They were white with black faces, the fur that coated their long limbs standing out at all angles. They sat hunched upon the branches of a dead tree around which their enclosure looked to have been built. With dark, intelligent eyes they watched the two figures moving below. As Krýl and the Witch drew nearer, the creatures began to grow agitated. They launched themselves from one branch to another, hooting as they tumbled through the air. They drew back their lips and showed their teeth. One reached between the bars and struck the cage with the flat of its hand.

In the gesture Krýl saw something that was more than the flailing of a distressed animal. To him it seemed the action of a man who has been imprisoned—a man frustrated with his confinement.

"Pay their antics no mind," said the Witch. "They howl and bare their fangs, but do not be taken in by such theatrics. They are more or less harmless."

Krýl looked up at the enclosure. The little creature that had struck the bars stared back at him, its long arm hanging limp before the cage.

"These little fellows represent the very last of their species," said the Witch. "The crystalline storms reduced their forest to splinters. By the time I had gathered up the survivors their home was not but a few acres across. Though they may protest, this cage has been their salvation."

Krýl turned from the simian. It hooted once as they made their way through the arch beside the cage, the sound doleful and haggard.

The corridor that led from the menagerie curved ever so slightly to the left. It was lit intermittently with glowing balls of light set in sconces that were in turn fastened directly to the stonework. Krýl squinted at the orbs as he passed, trying to determine what manner of flame could burn so bright and so steady. The Witch saw him scrutinizing the balls of light and laughed.

"They are from the old world. They will give off pure,

soft light for months on end. When they begin to fade they must be set in the sun for a day. Beyond that I can say very little about them, though I have taken several apart. The secret of their construction was lost centuries ago. Today they are each worth a king's ransom."

"Most everything here is." The words were out of Krýl's mouth before he had a chance to reel them back in. To his relief the Witch only smiled.

"You are not wrong. My most treasured possessions, however, cannot truly be valued. Not with gold...though I did pay handsomely for them. To me their value is intrinsic; they are a part of me. The first is just through here."

The Witch pushed an iron-shod door aside, metal and timber sliding inward without a sound. As it slid to, Krýl was struck by the smell and the sound of water trickling over stone and splashing into an open pool. He had heard such a sound only once before. In the Red Lands, water did not run out in the open. To find it one had to go underground, deep underground.

As he stepped within the chamber Krýl found himself picking his jaw off his chest for the second time in as many days. Drawing a deep breath of cool, moist air Krýl felt his sinuses open and expand. The sensation was exquisite.

"If they deign to speak to you do not believe what they say," said the Witch, tugging him inside the chamber and closing the door. "They may appear harmless, but that is far from the truth. Before I acquired them, they survived by luring men into their grotto. They would then rip the unfortunates apart and devour them."

Krýl's brow furrowed. The Witch smiled. It was the same expression she had worn before introducing him to sand wurm. Krýl glanced at the occupants of the grotto, then back at his hostess.

"They can speak?"

"They can." The Witch patted his shoulder. "Look."

There were five in all, waifish things that resembled pubescent girls. Their build was slight, their features soft, their skin the color of chrysocolla along their arms and legs, a pale buff around their breasts and belly. They lounged about a sunken pool fitted at its bottom with glowing spheres like those that lit the corridor. The orbs cast lightbirds along the ceiling, the walls, the naked limbs of the girls. As one they stared out at Krýl with large eyes that were as full and dark as polished onyx.

The Witch teased one coil of green hair around her index finger. "The nymphs will remain immobile until they have decided if you are predator or prey. Should they see you as the former then they will slink away and hide, the latter and they will approach. If you are fortunate, perhaps you will hear them sing."

Blinking away the spray from the waterfall that overhung the grotto, Krýl took a step towards the glass partition. The five figures continued to sit and stare, their hollow black eyes belying not the slightest hint of emotion. For a moment that seemed to stretch on for an age Krýl stood and regarded them. Then, ever so slowly, one of the creatures slid from where she had lain and entered the water. With a few quick strokes she traversed the pool, her shape silhouetted against the glowing orbs at its bottom. Once on the far side she raised herself gracefully from the water and stood.

Krýl watched the nymph closely as she approached the glass. She blinked several times, nictitating membranes flickering over dead, black eyes. Her stride was slow and deliberate, her narrow hips swaying. Biting at her lower lip with pearl-white teeth the nymph turned her head to the side. The Witch began to laugh.

"They know how to appeal to a man, yes? I have seen them attempt to seduce my soldiers a hundred times. Though I feed them regularly it seems they still feel the need to hunt."

The nymph stopped before the glass and cocked her hips. Her brows peaked plaintively and she ran one hand between her small breasts. The Witch's laugh rose and Krýl turned towards her. When he turned back the slender creature was pressed against the glass, her coquettish expression gone, her teeth bared. She hissed and struck the partition with the heels of her hands. Krýl stood his ground.

Again the nymph hissed, drawing back her lips to expose canines and premolars that were as long and sharp as those on an aýrs-hound. In response to the challenge Krýl felt the eukaryotic shell upon his back burst upwards. The jagged tendrils spread across his neck and shoulders, wrapping themselves around the sides of his face.

With a snarl, Krýl jerked towards the glass. The nymph recoiled and dove backwards into the pool. At this the Witch laughed all the harder.

"Oh my, she thought she had you. Alas, you are something far more dangerous than they had anticipated."

As one, the nymphs retreated towards the far side of their enclosure. There they huddled, showing their teeth and hissing. Krýl let the armor bristle a second time, extending fibrils towards the glass. The nymphs cowered further into their corner.

"Enough," said the Witch, her expression falling.

Krýl glared at her, then back at the nymphs. He drew a breath and tugged at the fungoid shell, forcing it from his face. As it went he felt his heartbeat slow, felt the familiar sensation of having had precious proteins siphoned by the armor.

Turning abruptly from the glass Krýl stalked from the grotto, pulled the door open. He paused in the open doorway and waited until his legs had stopped shaking. He then looked back over his shoulder at the Witch. With un-hurried grace she sauntered up beside him.

"Do not be cross, I meant you no harm. The nymph on the other hand…" She touched his shoulder and Krýl felt a spark leap from her finger.

"It takes a toll."

The Witch looked up at him. "The armor?"

"Yes."

"When it moves, when it grows?"

"Yes."

The Witch thought for a moment. "Then it is as much parasite as symbiote."

Krýl shrugged. "I don't know these words."

"It feeds upon you while at the same time protecting you, adding to you. It is a boon and a hindrance."

"That's putting it lightly."

The Witch laughed, patted Krýl's shoulder, then crooked her arm in his. "Come, I've many more wonders to show you."

Krýl followed as the Witch tugged him into the hall. Together they made their way up a spiraling flight of stairs and into another corridor. This led to more stairs that at last ended in a short hall. To Krýl's immediate left was another door made of thick wooden planks banded with iron. The Witch pushed it open with the tips of her fingers. As with its predecessor, the door swung inward without a sound.

As the door slid aside a sickly orange light followed by a wave of hot air struck Krýl full in the face. Instinctively he squinted and raised one hand to cover his eyes. The Witch tittered and shook her head. "You've spent too much time in the desert. Most men would have moved aside, but you face the light and the heat head on. Come, there is no blowing sand or crystal here."

With a swirl of her robes and a flash of her hip the Witch slipped into the chamber. A smile tugging at the corners of his mouth, Krýl followed.

To all appearances the chamber contained only a formation of crystals and sand set behind a thick pane of glass. They seemed to be growing from an oddly shaped lump of rock. When the lump of rock moved Krýl grunted and moved closer. His mind tried to reconcile what it thought it knew about crystal formations with what he was seeing. No satisfactory answer was forthcoming.

"For a man who has travelled the world you are rather easily overawed," said the Witch. She crinkled up her nose at him and giggled.

"I've seen the same things over and over again," said Krýl, leaning closer to the glass. "Sand. Crystals. The arse of the hýthric in front of me. When the fighting starts it's always the same. Blood and bone, men crying for their mothers. Crystals that can move don't figure into the life of a mercenary."

The Witch pursed her lips. "Blood and bone. How visceral. Lean in as close as you like. He doesn't move terribly quickly and seems to have no interest in eating anything but lizards."

Krýl moved closer.

The creature squatted amongst a cluster of stones veined with red crystal, like cirrus clouds cutting through the evening sky. The crystals that sprouted from the thing itself were of a similar type, though far more prominent. They jutted from its shoulders, elbows, knees, forearms, and shins. Descending from the crown of the creature's head was another line of crystalline growths. These ended just above the brow, directing the eye to the face below. Of the thing's countenance not much could be said. Krýl scanned the minimal features—the low brow, the lack of a nose, the sunken cheeks, the straight jaw. It had no lips, only a slit at the front of its face that served as a mouth.

"Is it—"

"It is," said the Witch. "A full deviant, though of a type few have ever seen. Over the years I had heard rumors of such things, but never lent them any credence."

The creature turned, the crystals on its back catching and reflecting the light of the overhead bulbs. These were responsible not only for the sickly orange light, but for the heat as well. Krýl turned his head to one side as the thing made its way towards the far end of the chamber. Its movements were slow, deliberate. Balancing on its knuckles it slouched over to the wall and attempted to lose itself within another cluster of rocks.

"I'm sure you've encountered your share of deviants with skin is like a reptile's and eyes protected by polarized membranes. They are adapted to the great deserts and the windswept mountains. They thrive where humans cannot, living in the most barren of environs. This fellow is far beyond even their superb adaptations. He comes from the Caldera, that furnace in which lives almost nothing and that only the extremely foolish or the extremely brave ever attempt to cross."

Krýl kept his eyes on the deviant, peering at it, watching as it drew into a ball. "Did you rescue it as well?"

"No," said the Witch. "I bought him from a slaver who had in turn purchased him from a band of deviants. The slaver said the deviants had made the crossing at the tail end of the hot season. After taking shelter from a storm they stumbled across this fellow quite by accident. He was wedged into a vein of crystal, unmoving, staring out at them. At first they thought he was a statue."

Krýl knelt before the enclosure. The creature opened its eyes and Krýl felt his scalp prickle. Even in the sallow glow of the spheres its eyes shone bright and golden.

"It is hot in here," said the Witch. "I do not wish to tarry."

Krýl turned towards her. She beckoned and he rose to his feet.

After a dozen paces the corridor turned sharply to the left. Set in the wall that now faced them was yet another door, this one as sturdy and thick as the last. Upon reaching it the Witch spun about, the look on her face one of almost childish glee. With eyes wide she said, "This one… this one is my favorite. She is like a living jewel, she—well you will just have to see for yourself."

With that the Witch flung the door wide.

Brilliant white light flooded the hallway. Krýl again threw his hand before his face, squinting into the glare. Through his fingers he could just make out the silhouette of the Witch as she made her way up a short flight of steps and onto a landing surrounded by walls of glass. The light shone through her flesh and robes alike, shifting as she moved, hinting at the skeleton beneath.

At the top of the stairs the Witch paused and looked back towards Krýl. With the white light glinting from her nearly fluorescent curls she extended one slender hand. "Come."

She lay on her side, stretched full length on a slab of carved marble. One leg was bent at the knee, her head resting in the crook of her elbow. Catching the sunlight that streamed through the glass panes overhead, her scales shone a deep, pearlescent white. Each graceful curve of her seemed to refract, to intensify that light, filling her enclosure to over-flowing.

Like the nymphs and the crystalline man she was a deviant. Though proportioned like a human woman, her features were reptilian. Her face was serpentine, her cheeks, chin, and brow bearing no small resemblance to that of a pit viper. Along the sides of her head were tympanic membranes instead of ears, and the back of her skull was swept into a pointed ridge.

Topping the stairs Krýl squinted at the deviant woman upon her marble couch. The Witch put a hand on his arm and the other on her chest. Out of the corner of his eye Krýl could see the rapid rise and fall of her breasts, the beat of her heart in the side of her throat.

"Is she not radiant?"

Krýl kept his mouth shut and nodded.

The deviant woman turned her head to the side, her tongue flicking from her lipless mouth. When she moved so did the light, tracing a pattern across the floor. The deviant woman tasted the air, eyes the color of fresh scar tissue staring from below limpid brows.

"Up with you, my darling," said the Witch.

Turning her head to the other side the deviant woman again gave a quick flick of her tongue. She propped herself up on one elbow, her mien becoming suddenly tense.

"No need for that," said the Witch. "Calm yourself, my love. Now, up with you."

In one fluid motion the deviant raised herself from the marble block and took several steps towards the glass. She paused, then continued on, her steps measured and careful. Krýl swallowed dryly.

The Witch made a soft sound in the back of her throat. "Do you see why she is my favorite?"

"I do."

"Many hours have I spent in this place gazing at her, the very epitome of beauty. It is such a cruel twist of fate that she cannot appreciate her own appearance. She is an albino, and blind."

Krýl frowned. "Cruel indeed."

The Witch saw his expression and clucked her tongue. "I enjoy her all the more because it. She belongs to me. I benefit from her presence, no one else. She does not need to see for I am blessed with sight. All she need do is exist."

For a moment Krýl did not respond. At last he lowered his arm and turned towards the Witch.

"Come now, don't be sullen," she said. "Do not think yourself one of these curios. They are none of them fully sentient. Were they able to hold congress with me, dine at my table, fill my bed, I would not have caged them so. As it is they are barely more than animals. I sequester them behind glass for their own safety as much as mine. Like the pride of simians in the menagerie I hold their lives in trust; feeding and caring for them where others would simply have slain them for trophies. Be it plant, animal, or mineral, I preserve it for posterity. In return I am afforded the opportunity to look upon them whenever I wish."

Krýl felt his jaw clench and unclench of its own accord. "Are there are more?"

The Witch turned towards the door. "Just one."

Four

From light into darkness.

As they moved further into the recesses of the keep the winding series of corridors grew dimmer. Fewer and fewer of the light-emitting spheres decorated the walls. The stone itself grew dull and gray; the floors showed signs of wear and buckling. Krýl remarked on this and the Witch made an annoyed gesture.

"This portion of the keep is older than the rest. In fact it predates all of the others. It has long been my intention to renovate this wing; however, I have not yet conceived a way of doing so without risking the loss of this final curio. He seems to be a part of the old keep, one with the ancient stones."

Krýl had only a moment to wonder what the Witch meant by this before they came to the fourth—or was it the one hundredth—door of dark wood banded with iron. It was set deep within the stonework, almost indistinguishable from the rest of the hall. Unlike the others, its hinges groaned when the Witch set her shoulder to it. Beyond was an empty room.

Reaching around the side of the doorframe the Witch plucked something from a low shelf. She gave the object three quick shakes and from between her fingers came a wan, purplish glow. In the weird light of the sphere the Witch's skin took on a sickly alien cast. When she smiled her teeth shone disconcertingly white.

"He cannot abide the light of day or that of the incandescent spheres. It causes him such pain. This does make viewing him a tad difficult. So we must rely on the mostly invisible spectrum, the ultraviolet."

The term was not familiar to Krýl, but he nodded anyway. The Witch's smile widened.

"There are things about the nature of light and dark, of particle and wave that would take hours to explain. Perhaps if you have the patience?"

Krýl snorted. This only made the Witch laugh.

"Would you like to know what other secrets I have locked

away in my memory?"

"I think I've seen enough for one day."

"But, my dear fellow, I have saved the best for last."

"An empty room is hardly going to be the highlight."

"Empty? I think not."

The Witch stepped into the room. Closing the door behind him, Krýl followed, half expecting to see a bat the size of a man hanging from the ceiling. He was surprised to see nothing but shadows.

It took several moments for his eyes to adjust. When he could at last make out the walls of the chamber he saw they were indeed bare. There were no furnishings, no decorations, nothing but flat, lifeless stone. Krýl turned in a complete circle, then back to the Witch.

In the light of the sphere he could clearly see the whites of her eyes, the irises reduced to floating spheres of black. Krýl wanted to ask the Witch what sort of trick she had played, but thought better of it. Obviously her little joke had not had its punchline yet. He would have to wait patiently while she had her fun, then endure her laughter at his expense. Forcing his features back into a mask of placidity, Krýl let his gaze drift from the Witch to the wall behind her. There he saw her shadow cast upon the rough stone and beside it his own.

Krýl's brow knit. He turned about and saw his shadow on the wall behind him. He then looked back to the Witch. There were two shadows behind her, yes, but the second could not be his. She held the sphere, therefore his shadow should extend behind him and hers would splash against the opposite wall.

Krýl took a step back.

The Witch grinned, raised the sphere higher. "You see him, yes?"

"I see something…but it makes no sense to me."

The Witch's nose crinkled. "What have you seen today that would make you think this last treasure of mine would suddenly be the one to make sense?"

Krýl shook his head. "What is it?"

"He," said the Witch.

"What is He then?"

"He was here when I inherited the keep…took it, rather. He haunted the ruined fortress that stood atop the crag on which we stand. I did not discover him until I had already begun construction on the newer portions of the fortress. He was the first to become a part of my collection."

Behind the Witch the shadow twitched, its edges fading then reforming. Krýl had to force himself not to recoil. "How do you know he is what you say he is? All I see is a shape against the far wall."

"When it pleases him, he speaks," said the Witch. "In the years since I acquired this fortress we have had many conversations. He has been around for a very long time and has seen a great many things. He is nearly as ancient as the stones themselves."

"What is he?"

The Witch raised one hand and fluttered her fingers. "He is a shade, or so he says. He exists in this world and yet he does not. He fluctuates between the temporal and the incorporeal, a thing that is not alive yet lives eternally."

"Was he once a man?"

The Witch shrugged. "Who can say?"

"Have you asked?"

"Of course, but on that subject he has remained frustratingly mute."

With that the Witch spun on her heel and made her way back to the door. When she reached it, she dropped the faintly glowing sphere in a declivity carved in the wall and pushed the door open. "I'm hungry. Join me?" She let the door shut behind her.

Shaking his head Krýl started for the door. After only a few shuffling steps he halted. A chill ran down his spine, raising gooseflesh along the back of his neck. Krýl sucked in a breath.

A voice as dry and cracked as old bone spoke from beside Krýl's ear. With it came with no hint of breath, only the quiet susurrus of empty aeons.

"Do you see?" asked the Shade. "You watch, but do you truly see?"

Krýl clenched his fists. Sweat beaded his forehead and temples. A single drop ran down his cheek and hovered poised along the line of his jaw.

"Think back."

The voice shifted, moved behind him. Krýl forced himself not to turn around.

"The gardens, the balcony...think."

Krýl thought. He thought back to the previous night when he had stood on the Witch's balcony overlooking her gardens. After being awakened he had waited and he had listened. He had seen and heard nothing.

"I saw you watching, saw you listen for the next scream. Tell me," said the Shade, "what do you think cries out so?"

When he at last spoke Krýl felt as though his mouth had been filled with sand. "I don't know."

"You will."

The armor twitched. Krýl felt it gnaw at him, begin to spread and grow.

The door opened just a crack, shedding a slanting bar of light across the floor of the empty room. The face that appeared against the doorframe belonged to the Witch. "Let us not dawdle," she said, "I am positively ravenous."

Krýl crossed the room in several shaky strides and stepped back over the threshold. As he closed the door behind him he glanced into the chamber. He could see no trace of the Shade.

THE GARDENS

———•●•———

One

"Oh, well placed!"

The Witch clapped her hands and grinned. Krýl returned her smile. It had been a fine shot. The sour expression on Kaalah's face said as much. Turning to the captain of the Witch's guard, Krýl cocked an eyebrow. Kaalah did not respond, but simply stood with arms crossed, glowering.

"You've a talent for this," said the Witch. The lucent woman flipped her mass of green curls over one shoulder and laid a hand on Krýl's arm. She beamed up at him. "And here you said the crossbow was not your forté."

Krýl shrugged and set the weapon on the long table that ran the length of the shooting gallery. On its weathered surface were laid even rows of quarrels, a winding mechanism, and several balls of wood wrapped in leather. The miniature catapult that flung these balls sat in front of the table, its throwing arm fully extended.

"They're useful," said Krýl, "but hardly a specialty."

"Cold steel in your clenched fist then?"

"I suppose."

The Witch pressed herself against his arm, tracing one finger over the place where the eukaryotic shell lay hidden beneath Krýl's tunic. "Or is it the armor that does your killing for you?"

Despite the Witch's softness, the Witch's nearness, Krýl rankled. The Witch, seeing that she had struck a nerve, pinched him and twirled away. Kaalah saw as much and chuckled. Krýl glared at him over one shoulder.

"Load it again."

"Do it yourself."

"Come now," said the Witch, "he's a guest."

Kaalah clenched his jaw, the muscles rippling beneath his trim little beard. Krýl saw as much and smirked.

Attaching the winding mechanism to the crossbow and fitting the toe of his boot into the stirrup at its front, Krýl winched the bowstring taut. When the loosing mechanism clicked into place he stood and gestured with his chin towards the miniature catapult. "More tension."

Kaalah ground his teeth and set about cranking back the arm of the device. When cords of muscle stood out on the soldier's neck and the miniature catapult's lever could be pulled no further Krýl said, "That'll do."

From off to one side the Witch tittered and bit at her thumbnail. It looked to Krýl as though she was enjoying winding both him and Kaalah like the catapult and setting them at one another.

Languidly, the Witch made her way towards the front of the gallery. She stood on the opposite side of the table, hips cocked, arms akimbo. "Ambitious," she said.

Krýl twitched up an eyebrow and raised the crossbow to his shoulder.

With a jerk Kaalah sprung the lever, hurling the wood and leather ball into space. Krýl watched as it soared out over the gardens, the arch of its trajectory carrying it high into the burnished copper sky. At the peak of its flight Krýl exhaled and gently squeezed the trigger of the crossbow. With a thump and a twang the bolt hissed after the ball. A breathless second later and it had sailed past, arching down towards the foliage below. With a shake of his head Krýl lowered the weapon.

"Too ambitious," said the Witch.

Kaalah, grinning, made his way from the shooting gallery. With a toss of her hair the Witch followed. Krýl set the crossbow on the bench, turned towards the gardens.

Below the shooting gallery stood a broad expanse of lawn. On the well clipped green lay the three balls he had pinioned with quarrels. The one errant shaft stuck in the earth several dozen yards from the ball it had missed. Beyond them stood a row of hedges, their thorny branches twisted into interlocking helixes. Further still stood a copse of trees amongst which could just be seen one of the Witch's other undertakings, a grotesque and oversized pod set on stalk made of interlaced vines. The sickly green of its dome showed through the branches of the helical trees, the mucous membrane that coated it reflecting the afternoon sun.

"It has grown hot," said the Witch from the far end of the gallery. "I no longer wish to stand out here roasting in the sun."

Krýl turned towards the keep. Ahead was the empty plaza that stood below the inner wall. The toothed shadows of the crenulations above were just beginning their march across the cobbles. The bloated red face of the sun seemed a long way from the western horizon. Krýl could see waves of heat rising from the broken silhouette of the mountains. Wiping at a trickle of sweat he stepped from beneath the gallery's awning and strode towards the door at the far end of the plaza.

Inside, the keep was cool, the light dim. It took several seconds for his eyes to adjust. Krýl blinked then made his way down the corridor after the Witch. Fist-sized spheres dotted the hall, their glow soft and unwavering. As she passed each of the spheres the Witch's skin caught the light, showing a lattice of veins and the translucent musculature beneath. Krýl quickened his pace.

"High tea," said the Witch without turning.

Krýl hastened to catch her up. "High what?"

"High tea," repeated the Witch. "That, I think, would make a fine end to the afternoon. Afterwards, I shall retire to my green houses. I have been neglecting my work and I am afraid my gardens are beginning to suffer for it. The gardeners take good enough care of the beds outside, but those most rare and delicate plants in my collection cannot go long without my attention."

Krýl nodded. In the weeks since his arrival he had learned more about horticulture than he had ever dreamed possible. Who knew plants required so much work? Those few growing things he had come across in the desert had always done well enough on their own.

"Black tea or green?"

Krýl thought for a moment then said, "Green."

The Witch cocked her head to one side. "No, I think black would be best."

Krýl shrugged. "Black it is then."

The Witch tossed her mass of green hair over one shoulder. "On second thought, I think I shall forgo the tea. Take a cup if you will, but I must tend to my gardens. There is work to be done."

So saying, she spun away from him. Gliding down a side corridor, her diaphanous gown trailing out behind her, the Witch disappeared from sight. Krýl took a step in the opposite direction, then stopped short. Kaalah stood at his elbow watching the last trace of the Witch vanish around a corner.

"Not long now."

Krýl raised an eyebrow.

"You've ceased to be entertaining," said Kaalah. "I give it a week before she either puts you out of the keep or locks you away."

Anger blossomed in Krýl, hot and unsparing. He felt his lip curl back from his teeth. "What would you know?"

Kaalah snorted. "I've seen it—half a dozen times, a dozen. All of the Mistresses' flings end the same. You'll become a part of her menagerie, or you'll be discarded."

Krýl felt a vein along his temple begin to pulse. "You're jealous."

The captain of the Witch's guard laughed. The sound was like hewn granite and equally as humorless. "The Mistress rules this keep and everything within view of its battlements. In her employ are hundreds of soldiers and servants. This fortress contains the finest collection of artifacts and oddities the world has ever known. Do you think she happed upon such treasures by chance? To keep her domain the Mistress must be ruthless, as much a bandit as a noble. To a woman like that you're nothing more than a passing fancy, a whim."

With a growl Krýl seized Kaalah by the front of his tunic and drove him back against the wall. Kaalah's head knocked against the stone and his eyes went momentarily blank.

"A whim, is that it? Then what are you? A servant, a slave

who may look but never touch? You're no more than a cur begging for scraps at her table!"

His eyes coming back into focus, Kaalah again began to laugh. He squirmed, gripped Krýl's wrists. "She had an affair with the deviant woman, the blind one that's locked away in a glass cage in the far tower. When they made love I could hear their cries echoing through the halls. Now she claims the deviant is little more than an animal. I can still remember them lying together in the sun, feeding each other fruit, and reciting poetry."

Krýl drew a sharp breath, blinked, relaxed his grip on Kaalah's tunic. The guardsman took advantage of this lapse and shot both arms up between Krýl's wrists. He pushed outwards, breaking the hold on his tunic, then rammed both hands into Krýl's chest. Krýl went staggering across the hall and knocked into the opposite wall. Kaalah was on him in an instant, his forearm at Krýl's throat and a dagger pressed against his belly.

"A dozen years ago she arranged a marriage with a war-lord from across the mountains to the west. He was a brute, a killer, a conqueror. He had seized more territory in four years of campaigning than all the other warlords in the west combined. To keep his armies at bay she took him to her bed and rode him until he begged her to stop. A year later he was dead, his men poisoned at the same feast where she stabbed him to death in front of two hundred dinner guests. After that no one dared challenge her." Kaalah smiled. "She still has his skull, stripped of flesh and carved with runes. It sits in her study. I've heard her speaking to it, laughing at it."

Pressure was exerted on the knife and Krýl felt blood run in a thin rivulet down his belly. From where it had lain dormant long his spine, the eukaryotic shell burst upwards. Jagged strands of armor coiled about his torso and middle, extending themselves up his neck and cheeks, down his arms and thighs. The knife pressing into his belly was expelled, falling to the floor with a clatter.

With a cry of rage Krýl knocked Kaalah's arm aside, then clamped his fingers around the man's throat. The guardsman's eyes went wide as he was lifted from the floor. Krýl held him at arm's length, dangling him in mid-air, his feet kicking wildly. Kaalah's hands went to his wrists, gripping the jagged shell. Twisting with all his might Kaalah tried to unclamp Krýl's fingers. He could no more break the mercenary's grip than he could move a mountain with his shoulder.

As Kaalah's face began to grow purple, his eyes bugging from his skull, Krýl remembered himself, his surroundings, his hostess. Abruptly, he loosed his grip and let Kaalah fall to the floor.

The guardsman sprawled on the stones, hacking and coughing. He gripped his throat, his tongue protruding from between his lips. Without waiting for Kaalah to recover Krýl strode down the hall. He half marched, half jogged until he was far enough within the bowels of the keep that he was sure no one was in earshot. He then raised his head and roared at the ceiling.

Fighting against the urge to chase down and slaughter Kaalah like a hog, Krýl drove his fist into the floor. The flagging cracked under the impact. Looking down he saw that the splintered stone around his knuckles spread out like a spider's web. He focused on the pattern, tracing the broken spiral with his eyes, mentally detaching himself from the armor's exhortations.

By increments the armor relented. Krýl slumped to the floor and laid his back against the wall. Sweat beaded his bald scalp, running down his cheeks and into his eyes. He wiped it away with the sleeve of his tunic. His heart still beating a furious tattoo, Krýl sat and listened until it eventually slowed.

Lowering his head he shut his eyes and breathed in the ancient, dry smell of the corridor. In his head Kaalah's words played over and over again. He tried to thrust them away, but they refused to go. Despite his best efforts to shut out what the guardsman had said, the prospect of being dismissed from the Witch's service was galling. She frightened him, infuriated him, made him mad with lust, yet all he wished to do was remain by her side.

Krýl pressed the heels of his hands into his eyes. He cursed, pulled his hands away, and watched as white and purple spots danced in his vision.

He hit the wall with the back of his fist, then hit it again for good measure. Getting to his feet, Krýl dragged himself further into the confines of the keep.

Two

Clouds scudded across the moon, throwing the gardens into shadow. Krýl stood on the balcony that looked out from the Witch's apartment, watching as the tracts of flowerbeds and groves of trees below were alternately obscured, then revealed. To his ears came the sounds of insects, the lonely cry of a night bird. He strained his ears listening for something else—a cry, a scream, a whimper. Beyond the insects and the night bird there was nothing.

Krýl looked back towards the darkened apartment, then again to the garden. In the distance there was a flutter of wings, the sound of rattling branches.

The Witch had been away for the whole of the afternoon. When he had enquired about her Krýl was informed that she would remain in her greenhouses for the duration and was not to be disturbed. Seeing the expression on his face the servant quickly withdrew, scuttling down a side passage.

Krýl had taken his supper alone, sitting on a high wall watching the last of the daylight slip from the sky. The crepuscular rays that followed shone like beacons in the gathering dusk. They filled the sky and burned the underbelly of the clouds. Krýl had watched them with a scowl on his face and an ache in his belly. After picking at his food he had thrown bits of his supper over the side of the parapet. Small winged creatures with flat, humanoid faces went darting after the pieces of bread and cheese. Krýl watched them squabble, shriek, and claw at one another. When his plate was empty he cast that over the parapet as well.

Now he again stood looking out over the Witch's garden, unable to sleep, thoughts scattered. He wanted to chase after her, to search the grounds and outbuildings.

To what end? The Witch had no use for another lickspittle like Kaalah.

"Have you discovered it, that place of blood, and terror, and screams?"

Krýl lashed out blindly at the source of the voice that had spoken in his ear. His fist connected with nothing, throwing him off balance. Catching himself against the marble railing, Krýl searched the darkness. The balcony and the chamber beyond were empty.

"Think," said the voice.

"Who—"

From out of the shadows a section of the darkness peeled away, stepping into the open. Krýl watched as it slid towards him, noiseless and insubstantial yet unmistakably there.

"You're the Shade, the thing leftover from the old keep." Krýl felt foolish even as the words passed his lips.

"The Shade," said the voice. "Yesss." It seemed to savor

the final syllable, rolling it around and drawing it out.

The section of shadow flitted across the open balcony, its progress almost too quick for the eye to follow. Krýl blinked, trying to focus on the illusory thing. He could not. Any attempt to look directly at it was brushed aside. Krýl settled for watching it out of the corner of his eye.

From one of the high parapets the night bird cried once, twice, and was silent.

Its edges drifting away in wisps, the Shade stood silently before Krýl. It seemed to vibrate and flicker, as if remaining in one place was an act of will.

"Think," said the Shade.

"Think of what?"

"Do not be dense," said the Shade. "I saw you. You stood, you watched, you listened."

Krýl shook his head. "I saw nothing, heard nothing."

"No," hissed the Shade. "You heard. Now think!"

"Stop speaking in riddles." Krýl bit off the words.

The Shade paused, drew back. It stood there flickering, its edges drifting away into the cool of the evening. Then, just as quickly as it had appeared, it was gone.

Krýl let his eyes wander over the face of the keep, up the balcony and towards the crenulated battlements above. The Shade was nowhere in sight. Shaking his head, Krýl went back to staring out at the garden.

The night bird made another attempt at singing, but only managed to sound forlorn.

Whatever the shadow had wanted it had not felt the need to elucidate. Krýl turned from the balcony and the garden below. Morning would come soon enough and he felt drained, his muscles sore. He had almost forgotten the strain the armor put on him. It was Kaalah he could thank for its momentary rise from dormancy.

Stripping off his clothes he laid himself on the pile of cushions that served for a bed. Outside the wind had begun to rise. He listened to it moan through the turrets and over the battlements until sleep finally took him.

She stood in the center of her enclosure, her head tilted towards the morning sun. It shone pale and wan though the glass paneled ceiling. Overhead, a high veil of clouds served to wash out the normally crimson light. In the early hours of the morning the wind had cleared the air of dust and other debris, leaving the sky a deep, rich blue glazed with white. To see blue sky was a rarity, one as uncommon as running water in the desert. Krýl thought it a pity that the deviant woman could see neither clouds nor the sky.

Krýl took another step towards the enclosure. The woman behind the glass made no sign that she had heard him. He took another step towards the barrier and halted. His own reflection stared back at him, a pale shadow cast over the image of the deviant.

Peering through the spotless single pane of glass Krýl traced the reptilian lines of the woman's face and neck, the graceful sweep of her clavicle. He watched the twitch of her nostril as she drew breath and the steady beat of her heart at the side of her throat. Perhaps feeling his eyes on her, the deviant woman shifted her weight, turning on her couch. Krýl was forced to look away as the sunlight was caught and reflected by her opalescent scales.

Blinking the brilliance from his eyes Krýl scratched at the back of his neck. He cleared his throat and waited to see if the deviant woman would acknowledge him. She did so by slipping off her couch and taking four deliberate and well-practiced steps forward. When she reach the partition she pressed her hand against the glass.

Krýl sucked in a deep breath.

The deviant woman turned her head as if to regard him. He looked into the pink irises and dilated pupils that stared sightlessly back at him. As she turned her head to the other side, nictitating membranes flickered from the corners of her eyes. Krýl gave a sympathetic blink.

"Would you speak with me?"

The deviant woman blinked again.

If the Witch was correct and this woman was little more than an animal he was wasting his time.

Krýl waited and watched as the deviant woman waited and listened. When at last he was convinced his errand had been pointless he made to turn away. With the first scuff of his foot the deviant woman thrust her head forward. Krýl watched as her tongue flitted from out of her lipless mouth, tasting the air. She then drew back and raised her chin.

"Speak." The sound of her voice was like the wind through a thorn bush.

Now it was Krýl's turn to pause. He collected his thoughts, fidgeted with the hem of his tunic, then said as deliberately as he could manage, "Were you lovers?"

The deviant woman smiled then, an act Krýl had not thought her kind capable of. She let her hand drop from the glass and tucked her arms under her breasts. "What is your name?"

"I—"

"Mine is Aílea."

Krýl turned his face away. "I'm called Krýl."

"You were here," said Aílea, "with her."

Krýl nodded in the affirmative before he remembered that she could not see him. "Yes, I was."

"Your scent," said Aílea, withdrawing her hand from the glass, "is that of a predator."

Krýl felt himself tense. The deviant woman took a half step back, her arms drawing tight about her middle.

Opening his mouth to speak, Krýl paused, then shut it again. He forced the corded muscles in his neck and back to relax. Aílea turned her head to one side, then back to the other, listening, tasting the air.

"Kalaah said something to me. He said that at first you and the Witch were lovers, that you fed each other fruit and that she recited poetry for you."

"Yes," said Aílea, "that is true."

"He said that when she tired of you, she caged you."

Aílea raised one arm, placed her hand over her heart. "I can smell the desert on you."

Krýl's brow knit. "Did she do this, cast you aside?"

Aílea stood very still, her serpentine features implacable. At last she said, "You're something unique. This is why the Witch invited you into her home. This is the same reason I was purchased."

Krýl cleared his throat.

"In my view, I am nothing special. But I cannot see, so how am I to know, truly? Others tell me that I am beautiful, that I should be adored, revered. This means nothing to me. The adoration of those who have owned me has brought me only seclusion and loneliness. To them I'm like a rare gem that must be hidden away lest others should covet it."

Krýl felt his expression darken.

Aílea tilted her head to the side. "The Witch will be yours, and you will be hers. At least for a time."

"And after that?"

Aílea spread her hands and took several steps back from the glass. Her scales again caught the light and shone a brilliant white. Then she was in shadow, her body concealed by an overhanging beam. Krýl watched as she slunk into a corner and hid herself there in the cool and the dark. He then turned and strode from the chamber.

The day was long when the Witch at last wafted through the gallery, her head up and her fingers steepled in front of her. Krýl watched as she alternately appeared then disappear behind the columns that ringed the courtyard where he stood, sword in hand. He was covered in sweat, the remains of a practice dummy chopped to bits at his feet.

Krýl raised his hand, but the Witch disappeared around a corner and was lost from sight. With a shrug he set off after her.

Through the sparse windows of the keep the westering sun shone red as blood. The Witch waded into these crimson motes, her stride unvaried. Krýl tried his best not to run, but at times was forced to jog to keep up with her. When at last he was within a few paces of the Witch she turned her head and glanced at him over one shoulder. He remained just a step or two behind until she passed into her private apartments.

Krýl stopped in the doorway, chest rising and falling, hearing his own heartbeat in his ears.

She stood with her back to him, her gaze fixed on the open casement that led onto the balcony. A hot wind from out of the west lifted the curtains. Beyond, the distant line of the mountains was an umber smudge against the charred horizon.

"Remove your tunic."

Krýl hesitated for a moment, then set his sword to one side. Slowly he began to unlace the ties at his chest. When they came free he looked up to see the Witch standing before him. Krýl drew the sweat-soaked cloth over his head and dropped it to one side.

She watched him for a moment, eyes narrowed.

"What?"

The Witch laid one hand on Krýl's chest and hooked the other around the back of his neck. He felt her fingers probe at the patch of eukaryotic shell that still clung to the base of his skull. It twinged and writhed as her nails dug into it.

Pulling herself in close, the Witch licked at a trickle of sweat that clung to his jaw. Krýl felt her tongue on his skin as her hand slid down the front of his trousers.

Then, just as suddenly, she withdrew.

Krýl lifted his chin and looked down his nose at her. The Witch gazed back at him, her eyes searching. Not finding whatever it was she sought, she turned away.

"Where've you been?"

The Witch glanced at him out of the corner of one eye. "My gardens. I told you before I left."

"For a night and a day?"

The Witch did not reply. Krýl took a step towards her and reached out a hand. Grasping her upper arm he made to turn her around. Instead, the Witch pivoted in the opposite direction and lashed out with her nails. Krýl jerked back as they raked his cheek.

"You do not inquire about my whereabouts!" hissed the Witch. "I am mistress here! I come and go as I please."

Krýl stood with one hand to his cheek, glaring at the lucent woman. Behind them the curtains billowed and snapped as the wind swept in over the balcony.

"I was concerned," said Krýl, hearing the petulance in his voice even as he spoke.

The Witch scoffed. "What have you to be concerned about?"

"You were here one moment, then gone the next—"

The Witch raised a hand. "Where I go and what I do in

my own keep are no concern of yours."

"They are," said Krýl, color rising in his cheeks. Stepping forward he again took the Witch by the arm. She slashed at his shoulder and he winced as her nails drew blood. He ignored it. Crushing her to him, Krýl gripped the Witch by the hair and pulled her head back. Looking down into the delicate contours of her face he saw only enmity and bile.

"Do not dare to presume."

His lip curling from his teeth Krýl thrust the Witch from him. Snatching up the sword from where he had dropped it, he strode to the door. It was the Witch's tone that stopped him, the hot anger he felt turning suddenly cold. "I have not given you permission to leave."

Krýl stood with one hand on the door, the other gripping the scabbard of his saber. He remained motionless, feeling the Witch's eyes burn into his back.

"Remove your trousers."

Krýl turned. The Witch, her robes parted and blowing in the same breeze that moved the curtains, gestured towards the floor. Krýl glared at her.

"Now."

Allowing his sword to drop to the tiles with a clatter, Krýl stripped off his boots. He reached for the ties at his waist, then stopped.

The Witch ran a hand through her hair, tossed it back over her shoulder, and shrugged off the last of her robes.

"Go on."

Krýl unlaced his trousers, stripped them off.

Raising one finger the Witch beckoned. With slow, even steps Krýl made his way across the tiles until he once again stood in front of her. Unblinking, she stared up at him, lips pursed, breasts rising and falling. Over the scent of the desert and his own sweat Krýl could smell something else, like the musk of a rare flower.

"Your garden, does it require a hand so strong? Can you simply command the flowers to grow one by one?"

The Witch looked into his eyes, again searching. This time she found what it was she sought and smiled. "They do as they are told, like all of my subjects."

"I am a guest," said Krýl, "not one of your pets."

Sliding a hand down his chest and over the rigid contours of muscle and scar tissue she said, "You are not so different from them."

Seizing her under the arms Krýl heaved the green-haired women onto the pile of cushions in the far corner of the chamber. She struck and bounced, landing with limbs splayed. He was on her in an instant, pinning her beneath him. Writhing and thrashing, the Witch fought against his weight. Krýl held her firmly in place.

"Go on, speak to me as though I were one of your flowers, your thorn bushes." Veins stood out on Krýl's face and arms as he struggled to keep the Witch from breaking free. "Sing me a lullaby; coax me to grow."

"At a word," hissed the Witch, "I could have you flayed alive."

"And what makes you think I would go willingly? I could do all manner of things with you before the guards arrive."

"You err," said the Witch, growing suddenly still.

Krýl released his grip.

As swift and agile as a lýr-cat she was out from under him and throwing one leg across his chest. Krýl made to grab hold of her wrists, but the Witch was too quick. She pinned his arms above his head and forced him into the cushions.

Straddling him, green tresses falling over his face and chest, the Witch held perfectly still. Krýl could feel the blood in her veins, coursing fast and hot. Her normally translucent skin was flushed, nearly opaque.

"I could have you hung from the walls, your guts about your ankles, or trampled by hýthric. I could have your eyes put out, then have you dumped in the nymph's enclosure. They would toy with you for days, removing pieces of you and eating them at their leisure. Your death would be long in coming."

Slowly Krýl forced one hand up from the cushions. With the Witch's fingers still wrapped about his wrist he took her by the throat. "And I could choke the life from you before you had a chance to scream."

The Witch drew a deep, shuddering breath.

"And then?"

"And then I would let the carapace do its work."

The Witch gasped and removed her hands from his wrists. Krýl felt her swallow as he tightened his fingers around her throat.

"It would feed, yes?"

"It would drive filaments into your arteries and cut away bits of your flesh. It would harvest you one morsel at a time."

The Witch moaned, shuddered, began to work her hips back and forth.

"The carapace would pull the flesh from your bones, split them for their marrow, hollow them out and leave them in the dust."

She lowered herself onto him then, drawing his other hand to her throat. He tightened his grasp as she again began to move.

"It would use every last bit of you."

The Witch's cries drifted past the billowing curtains and out into the gathering twilight. Her voice rose and fell, rose and fell until the stars came out and the wind turned cold.

Three

It was near dawn when the shadows again spoke. Krýl sat bolt upright, his hand groping for a sword that wasn't there. Beside him the Witch lay with her back turned, her knees drawn up, her breath steady and shallow.

"You have learned nothing."

Krýl's brow knit as a piece of the night detached itself and drifted towards him. He watched the Shade glide across the marble floor, skimming around stray patches of moonlight. When it was by his side he rose to meet it. "What do you want now?"

"I want you to think."

With a shake of his head Krýl turned away. He padded across the tiling until he found the chamber pot that stood in one corner. Flipping the lid aside with one toe he urinated into the basin. Behind him he heard the Shade make an odd choking noise.

"You want me to think?" asked Krýl over his shoulder. "On what should I ruminate?"

"On the keep, on the gardens, on the soil."

"Should I contemplate the moon, the stars, and the heavens while I'm at it?" Finishing, Krýl flipped the lid of the pot shut and turned about. The night air was cool on his skin. He squinted into the darkness, hunting for the Shade. A moment later it was again before him, its outline smudged and wavering.

"Think," said the Shade. "Why would screams echo through the garden?"

"The world is unkind," said Krýl. "I've heard screams on many nights and in many places."

"In this place there is no cause for screams unless the Witch decrees it."

Krýl's lips pressed themselves into a thin line. He crossed his arms over his chest. "No more riddles. I can't stomach them."

"The greenhouses—go there. Seek their lowest point. See why such a foul humor was hers upon returning." With that the creature was gone, melted away into the darkness. Krýl let his rebuttal die in his throat.

Across the room the Witch sighed and rolled over in her sleep. Krýl could see her thigh and the turn of her hip in a puddle of moonlight. They were sleek and smooth. Fighting the urge to return to the heap of cushions, he followed the beam of moonlight out past the casement. The memory of the cry that had risen over the gardens then fallen suddenly quiet was fresh, and raw, and made his stomach hurt.

As quickly and quietly as he could, Krýl gathered up his clothes and slipped from the apartment. As the door latched behind him the Witch again sighed and stretched, her translucent flesh limned against the cushions.

"Take a walk."

The guardsman looked up at Krýl, then back down the hall. He swallowed, shifted his weight from one foot to the other. When he looked back at Krýl his expression was unsettled, one eye squinted half shut.

"I can't do that."

"You can and you will."

The guardsman shook his head. "She'll have me killed for abandoning my post."

"Then stay where you are, but let me pass."

"I can't do that either."

"And why not."

"She'll—"

"—have you killed," Krýl finished.

The guardsman, though plainly ill at ease, stood his ground. Krýl couldn't blame the man. He had stood watch on hundreds of nights in hundreds of camps. The penalty for dereliction was never light, even if your post was in a lighted corridor and not a siege trench.

Krýl squinted up into the glowing sphere just over the guardsman's head. It gave off the same unwavering light as all the others in the keep. "I don't want to see you hanged any more than you do, but I'm still going through that door. You can either ignore the fact that I passed this way, or I can tell the Witch you refused a request from one of her guests. Your choice."

The guardsman sagged in his armor. He shook his head, looked to one side, and gestured Krýl forward.

"Smart fellow."

As the door clicked shut behind him Krýl thought he heard the man mutter a short prayer.

Mounting the stairs two at a time, Krýl wound his way up and up until he came to the door that led to Aílea's enclosure. There he hesitated.

"Foolish."

Krýl turned about, took three steps back down the spiral stair, then stopped. He shook his head. He had come this far, why stop now?

Beyond the door everything was moonlight and shadow, hard lines broken only by the figure standing at the center of her enclosure.

At the back of his mind Krýl felt the fungoid shell twitch. It smelled fear. He ignored it and took a step forward. "Aílea."

The deviant woman stood stock still behind her wall of glass. She was like a statue set with thousands of gemstones, each having caught a tiny spark of the moon.

Krýl stepped to the glass. "Aîlea."

"I do not think that you are lost."

"No, I'm not lost."

"You are not lost, yet you are not where you should be."

Krýl crossed his arms. "I'm where I want to be."

The deviant woman came forward then, careful steps bringing her to within a foot of the glass. She gazed at Krýl out of her sightless eyes, her tongue flicking in and out, in and out. "She will not be pleased."

"She doesn't need to know."

Aîlea turned her head from one side to the other. "Why are you here? No one comes to see me after the sun has set, not even the Witch."

"Then she's doing herself a great disservice."

Aîlea did not respond, simply stood and waited.

"I wanted…" Krýl shook his head, uncrossed his arms, then crossed them again. "I wanted to talk."

The deviant woman's tongue waved at him, then withdrew inside the graceful curve of her mouth. "You wanted to talk."

"Yes."

"Why?"

"Why not?"

Aîlea took a step back. "Just as no one comes to me after the sun has set, no one comes to me simply to talk. The Witch desired to gaze upon me, to make love to me, to possess me. I think you have come to kill me and to eat me."

Krýl almost laughed. He caught himself at the last moment. "No, I haven't come to kill you and to eat you."

The deviant woman shifted sideways, her tongue waving, waving at him. "I can smell the thing on you, in you. It covets."

Krýl nodded. "Yes, it covets. It covets you like it covets

all living things. It didn't drive me here, didn't tell me to kill you. I came of my own accord. As I said, I want to talk."

Backing herself away from the glass partition and into a corner, Aílea tried to make herself small. Krýl moved in her direction and the deviant woman recoiled.

Frowning, Krýl stopped. "I haven't come here to kill you. I've already said as much."

"In the day you were…different."

"Different?"

"Yes."

"How?"

"You were just a man with something wriggling around inside him. Now the thing that is inside of you speaks. I can hear it moving beneath your skin, reaching for me."

"It knows that you're afraid." Krýl stepped up to the glass, leaned upon it with his forearm. "It's like an aýrs-hound. If it can smell that you are afraid, it will begin to think of you as prey."

"So you're saying all I need do is banish my fear and it will no longer think of me as food? How simple."

Krýl tapped twice upon the glass. "I don't think of you as food. That is what's important."

"Somehow I am not reassured."

As an errant patch of clouds slipped past the keep a shaft of moonlight, as clear and cold as eternity, touched the deviant woman's foot. She pulled the foot back into the shadows.

"If you do not wish to talk, to hold a conversation, then perhaps you can answer a question for me."

Aílea shook her head. "I am naked, and I am alone, caged like an animal. What answers could I possibly give you?"

"You've been here how long, one year? Two?"

"Four," said the deviant woman, pressing herself further

against the wall.

"Four years…" Krýl tapped on the glass again.

"Do not do that."

"Sorry."

Aílea, her body bent forward by the sloping angle of the wall, pressed her palms to the stonework and raised her head. "The first year I spent with the Witch, always at her side. The second saw her slowly lose interest in me. By the third I was…sequestered."

Krýl ran a hand over his bald scalp. "In that time did the Shade ever come to you?"

Silence.

Aílea remained pressed against the wall. Krýl watched the rise and fall of her breasts, the flicker of her tongue.

"He came to you?"

"He did."

"What did he say?"

"He told me to think."

Aílea was again silent.

Krýl shifted position, drew back his fingers to tap on the glass, then stopped himself.

"He said the same to me." Aílea slipped from the shadows, stepped into a crystalline shaft of moonlight.

"The Shade said I should look to the gardens, to the soil. It made no sense."

Aílea came forward, again moving to within a foot of the glass. "Did he tell you to seek the lowest point?"

"He did."

Aílea raised a hand to her mouth, bit at one nail.

"What is it?"

"He came to me, not long after I was brought here. He spoke to me as he spoke to you. When I told the Witch what the Shade had said she laughed."

"Why?"

"She does not believe that he can leave his dark little room. She thinks she has him caged as well as she has caged the rest of us."

"The rest of us?"

Now it was Aílea's turn to stifle a laugh. "The birds, the reptiles, the primates, the nymphs, the stone man. You remember them, surely?"

Krýl chuckled to himself. "I can be dense, but yes, I remember them."

"The Witch has us all locked away, but not as well as she may think. The Shade moves about at will. When I first came here he implored me to seek the gardens, as he did you. I told him I was blind. He did not seem to understand."

"There are a great many things he doesn't seem to understand. Perhaps it's been too long since he could be counted amongst the living."

"Perhaps."

Aílea put a hand to the glass. "I do not know what the Shade meant. I am sorry."

Krýl shrugged. "Not to worry."

"If I knew anything at all I would tell you."

"What about the nymphs, the stone man? Would they be able to tell me anything?"

"They will not speak. I do not think the stone man is capable, though I do not think he is as simple as the Witch says. The nymphs only wish to fill their bellies. They will entreat with no one."

Krýl turned from the partition. "I'm sorry to have disturbed you."

"Stay."

Krýl cut his stride. "I'm sorry?"

"Please." Aílea pressed her other hand to the glass.

"I thought you didn't care for me."

"I can no longer hear it."

"The armor?"

"Yes. It has gone silent."

Unconsciously Krýl reached around the back of his neck to pick at the dormant shell. "It's never been this quiet. The Witch touched it and it withdrew."

"Withdrew?"

"Normally it covers me from neck to toe."

Aílea put a hand over her heart. Krýl chuckled.

"Tell me about it, this armor of yours."

"Alright," said Krýl.

For the second time since he had known her, Aílea smiled.

Four

Krýl swung and a bit of the straw man fell away. Using the momentum of his swing to reset his blade, he again extended his arm, flicked his wrist, and scored a cut. This Krýl did three more times up the dummy's right side, then shifted his focus to its left. When he had made another five cuts and straw drifted through the air in a lazy flurry, he stepped back.

To one side a group of guardsmen, their heads together, spoke in low tones and gestured towards him. Krýl caught a nod of approval out of the corner of his eye. Wiping sweat from his brow, he again lined up before the dummy.

Another flick of the wrist and the saber struck out, scored the dummy's chest. Another flick administered another cut, and then another. Krýl followed these with a hard reset of his stance and a ruinous gash to the dummy's abdomen. Straw entrails splashed across his boots and the legs of his trousers.

One of the guardsmen gave out a single syllable laugh and clapped his hands. The others crossed their arms and nodded. Krýl allowed himself a half smile.

"He's dead," said the guardsmen who had laughed. "You've killed him."

"Fearsome fellow," said another. "Glad to be rid of him."

Krýl snorted.

"Why don't you add a friend for him? See if you can kill two straw men at once?"

Glancing towards the guardsman, Krýl then turned back towards the training ground. Set to one side, along a red stone wall, stood a row of dummies. They were fastened to poles, their straw limbs wrapped in cheap rags. He looked back towards the guardsmen. "Two of them? Don't know if I can manage."

The first of the guardsmen held up two of his fingers.

"I may not survive, but if that is what you wish to see…"

The guardsman smirked, held his fingers higher, gave them a wiggle.

Krýl retrieved two of the dummies from the wall and set them in the middle of the training ground. Underfoot the sand was hot, its surface covered with bits of his first victim. Overhead the sun was near its zenith, its sanguine light filtered by a pall of dust. Krýl glanced up, then back down at his feet. He set his stance and shook out his arms.

Swing right, then swing left. Cut up, down, up, down. Alternate from one target to the next. Fist, wounds to disable. Second, blows to kill. Third; dismemberment. Just to be certain.

When Krýl was done both dummies lay in tatters. The guardsman gave him a cursory round of applause. Krýl affected a mock bow.

"Sloppy."

Krýl looked up, then straightened. His expression fell.

Stepping from the covered walk, Kaalah made his way past the guardsmen to the edge of the sand. All three of the soldiers got to their feet and went to parade rest.

"Your form," said the captain, "leaves much to be desired. Your manners even more so."

Krýl glared at the man. Kaalah met his gaze.

"I've been instructed to give you a message."

Krýl adjusted his grip on the hilt of his saber. Kaalah saw as much and smirked.

"You want to use that thing on me?"

"Crossed my mind."

"You wouldn't stand a chance."

"I've fought in hundreds of engagements, dozens of campaigns. I think I know what I'm doing."

"Hacking your way through a line of retreating regulars is much different than facing a man one-on-one."

"Is it?"

Kaalah nodded. "To beat a man on equal terms is not something a mercenary like you would understand." He made a dismissive gesture. "Besides, you've been letting that thing attached to your back do all your killing for you. I doubt if you could stand against a real opponent, let alone one who knows what he is doing."

Krýl reached to one side, picked up his scabbard, and rammed his blade home. "Did you come here to try and goad me into a fight, or did you have a message for me?"

The captain of the Witch's guard smiled, crow's feet appearing at the corners of his eyes. "The Mistress has bid me inform you that until further notice you are to be restricted in your movements. You are no longer permitted in the upper keep after dark. This includes the menagerie and the far tower."

A hand closed around Krýl's heart. Kaalah's smile widened and he felt its grip tighten.

Raising one finger and wagging it at him, Kaalah said, "You should not have gone exploring. This was rude. Such poor manners the Mistress cannot abide." Then his back was turned and he was striding away. Krýl watched him go, then glanced at the three guardsmen. They averted their eyes and, one by one, slunk from the training ground.

Palming sweat from his eyes and shaking his head, Krýl moved in the opposite direction. He stopped just outside the ring of sand.

"Kaalah."

Krýl heard the captain scuff to a halt.

"To first blood."

Silence followed his words. Then a gradual intake of breath and a single syllable, "No."

"Naked steel and naked flesh. No armor."

Again there was a pause. "No."

"Is this simple cowardice on your part or is your mistress calling. Does she have another errand for you to run? Perhaps there's a kitchen boy who has earned a beating for burning a loaf of bread?"

Krýl turned towards the training ground in time to see Kaalah do the same.

"To first blood."

The captain of the Witch's guard drew his saber and advanced to the middle of the training ground. With a smile, Krýl cast aside his scabbard, raised his own blade, and moved to meet him.

Kaalah did not hesitate, did not wait for a formal start to the duel. When Krýl was within range he struck. His blow was expert; moving past Krýl's guard he drew a line of blood along one shoulder.

"First blood."

Kaalah wiped the thin streak of red from the edge of his saber, sheathed it, and marched back towards the keep. Krýl watched him go, feeling the sting of the cut as his sweat touched it.

Stalking back the way he had come, kicking up great gouts of sand as he went, Krýl retrieved his scabbard. When he had again sheathed his blade he left the training ground. Skirting the keep's inner curtain, Krýl emerged at the fringe of the gardens. He stopped short just shy of the entrance to the soldier's barracks.

Hanging from the wall above the bronze door was the corpse of a man. Though its face was swollen, its eyes bulging, Krýl recognized the soldier that had stood guard at the foot of the stairs that lead to Aílea's enclosure.

Wiping sweat from his eyes, Krýl cursed, turned on his heel, and walked away.

Five

Sleep did not come. Krýl tossed, Krýl turned, but Krýl remained awake. He tried counting the stars visible through the narrow window in the chamber he had been allotted. He stopped after eight. He turned to exercise, working himself into a lather then falling back into bed with the hope that exhaustion would carry him off. It did not. So Krýl sat on his bunk and brooded.

"And what, exactly, is this meant to accomplish?

In the stony silence of his cramped little room the words seemed alien, out of place. Krýl let them trail away.

Wadding up the bedclothes he beat them unmercifully

with his fists. At this latest surge of activity the armor wriggled, tried to spread. Krýl quit his assault on his blankets and backed against the wall.

Pressed against the cool stone he could feel the fungoid shell moving just beneath his skin. He forced it back, back until it quit its squirming.

"Why?"

The voice from out of the darkness took Krýl by surprise. He jerked back from the wall. When he realized that it was the Shade who had spoken, he cursed himself for letting it get the better of him yet again.

"Why?"

The shadows beside the bed elongated and slithered across the wall. They formed into the semblance of a man no more than a yard from where Krýl stood.

"Go away."

"Why do you not seek answers? You keep vigil over the gardens. Do you not wish to know?"

"It's been weeks. Things change. Now go away."

The Shade twitched and flickered. Krýl took a step back, moving towards the center of the narrow room.

"Screams in the night no longer interest me."

"They should."

Krýl shook his head. "What does someone yelling their lungs out in the dark have to do with me?"

"Everything."

"Bollocks."

The Shade jerked, faded, brought itself back to the corporeal. "Look to—"

"—the gardens, I know. The deviant woman said you told her as much. And thanks to my conversation with that poor girl locked in the tower a man died. Besides, what's so important that you need others to go creeping around the Witch's garden for you?"

"You will see."

It faded then, slipping back into the darkness, dissolving into nothing. Krýl took a swipe at the place where it had been, then cursed and spat.

Pushing off from the wall he walked to his cot, sat down heavily. For several moments he sat with his elbows on his knees and his head in his hands. He listened to the drone of insects in the distant gardens and the thud of his own heart. At length his raised his head and looked around the room.

The door to the chamber wasn't locked, but a guard been posted just down the hall. Krýl thought this either very foolish, or surpassingly clever. Not that either foolishness or cleverness was going to stop him.

Getting to his feet, Krýl snatched his clothes from where he had tossed them, dressed, then pushed the door open.

Inside the greenhouse the spheres that hung from the ceiling gave off not only a deep yellow-orange light, but heat as well. Here, even in the dead of night, it was as bright and hot as midday. Bright, and hot, and humid as well. It was as though a cloud had been driven to earth. Krýl breathed it in and felt his sinuses open. The sensation was pleasant, at least until he started sneezing.

When the fit had passed, Krýl glanced around. The plants did not seem to have noticed.

Pleasant though it was to be surrounded by so much moisture, Krýl knew he could not simply stand around breathing in and out. He was an interloper, a foreign body in this sealed environment. Glancing from side to side he chose a direction at random and began following the rows of seedlings that stretched the length of the room.

From the outside the greenhouses did not look to be

particularly large or intricate. In fact, they appeared to be little more than a few glass-walled buildings nestled amidst low shrubs and stands of bladed succulents. Once inside, Krýl discovered they were a labyrinth. There were corridors and passageways hidden from the outside by cleverly fashioned panels and partitions. Trap doors led away to hidden basements in which burned orbs of a dozen different hues. In some of these subterranean grottos the light and heat was intense; in others it was wan and cold. Plants, thousands of them in all stages of growth, were laid out in neat rows or clustered on tables. Complex irrigation systems fed water to the herbage through copper or ceramic pipes. A few of the rooms contained plants that floated in shallow pools, their roots dangling in the clear water. In one of these bobbed a flotilla of orchids, their broad white petals tipped with crimson. To Krýl it appeared as though they had been dipped in blood.

In every chamber he unlatched grew a multitude of mesophytes, hydrophytes, xerophytes, or epiphytes. Krýl recognized fruit-bearing trees and bushes, beds of tubers and root vegetables. In some of the chambers there were plants that could kill, plants that could cure, plants that could separate a man from his mind while they siphoned the moisture from his flesh. Buzzing about them all was an army of insects. Confined to each individual room, the chitinous little creatures industriously shuttled pollen about or kept parasites at bay. Krýl batted them from his face as he passed, hoping that he had not allowed too many to escape each time he opened a new door.

At last he came to a chamber that was partially cut into the side of the mountain on which the keep stood. The ceiling and the upper half of the walls were made of frosted glass, the lower half chiseled into the bedrock. Broader and taller than the previous rooms, it contained fully grown trees and succulents that stood to a height of nearly three stories. Here the air was less suffused with moisture. To Krýl it felt almost like the world outside. At the far end of the chamber stood a copse of thorny, sharp-smelling trees. Through their branches he saw something familiar, something that made him cringe.

Nestled amongst the trees and succulents was a spheroid shape, its sides a sickly green and glistening with mucus. Krýl had seen several like it before, half hidden by trees or shrubbery. The only example he had seen up close had been on the day he arrived. The Witch had been so very pleased with the grotesque thing, though for the life of him Krýl could not tell why.

Repulsed though he was by the sight of that strange growth, Krýl made his way towards it through the succulents and around the trunks of the trees. Pushing through a stand of bushes he found himself at its base, looking up into the gills that ringed its underside. In the back of his mind he felt the symbiote begin to squirm.

Krýl raised his arms in an exaggerated shrug, then let them drop to his sides. Whatever the Shade had been prodding him towards seemed to be nothing more than an extension of the gardens he had already seen. And, much to his chagrin, this was the furthest point in the green-house complex. He had found nothing and to get out he would have to somehow retrace his steps.

With a sigh Krýl turned his back on the bulbous growth and started for the door. He glanced back once, feeling as though the hybrid thing was staring a hole in his back. He had taken another half dozen steps before he realized there was a trapdoor cut into the sandstone just behind the growth.

Krýl stopped and turned slowly around. One more door

then. He had come this far, after all.

The door was narrow, made of a heavy, dark wood, and secured with an iron bolt. To Krýl it seemed too small for a man of his size. He hesitated, then reached for the latch anyway.

At the back of his mind the armor let out a scream. Krýl pulled his hand from the latch just as the fungoid shell began to writhe in earnest. Spreading out from where it had receded along Krýl's neck and back, he felt tendrils creep over his shoulders and wrap themselves around his middle. He winced and tried to force the thing back into hiding. It refused to go.

When the armor had spread from the base of his skull to the soles of his feet, Krýl let out the breath he had not realized he had been holding. He steadied himself, felt its gnawing at his insides subside.

"Was that necessary?"

The armor did not bother to respond.

Grasping the bolt in one hand Krýl pulled. The door did not budge. He tried again. The result was the same.

Extending one long, thin tendril from the shell that covered his wrist, Krýl slipped it between the door and its jam. Using the extended nerve endings the armor allowed him, Krýl felt about until he located the latching mechanism. A few seconds' work and the lock was sprung.

From out of the darkness behind the door came the smell of rot. It made an assault on Krýl's nose, gagging him even as he turned away. In the back of his mind he felt the armor both urge him forward and urge him to flight. Whatever the eukaryotic shell had scented reminded it of a meal to be scavenged and of danger to be avoided. It could not settle on a single course of action. Krýl made the decision for it and slipped through the door.

Inside the chamber the air was stifling and thick. Damp and rot hung like a miasma, forcing Krýl to breathe through his mouth. He hung in the dark, suspended by his hands for a moment, then dropped.

On reaching the floor his foot squelched in something sticky and wet. Krýl took a step back and put his heel in something else equally as noisome.

"Fuck…"

A few feet beyond the door and the light from above no longer penetrated the gloom. Krýl could only guess at what he had stepped in. Reluctantly, he instructed the armor to make a light. In response it extended a tendril at the end of which a small bundle of filaments glowed a phosphorescent blue.

Gazing into the small halo of light Krýl's face contorted. In the center of the chamber stood a heap of compost, the vegetable matter slick with decay. In the middle of the pile lay a pod like the one in the room above. It was crumpled and smashed, its sides split. Protruding from the gash was a human hand.

Seemingly of their own accord Krýl's feet moved him closer. Squinting, he raised the lighted filaments.

Something crunched underfoot.

Lifting his foot Krýl examined the ankle deep muck in which he had trod. Poking from the greenish-black fluid was something sharp and white. He looked closer.

Scattered amongst the vegetable matter was a motley collection of bones. They stuck out at odd angles, a jumbled mass that had settled in on itself. Further up the mound could be seen several skeletons partially denuded of flesh. To Krýl they looked like an ossein waiting to be rendered down. Over it all roamed fat, white snails as long as his arm. Blindly they scaled the heights of the mound, oblivious to the stench or the lack of light. They crawled and feasted, leaving in their wake trails of slime that made the rot glisten in the blue glow of the filament.

Krýl tried his level best not to vomit.

The hand that protruded from the pod itself looked somewhat fresher than the rest of the heap. The fingers, however, were too thin, the flesh too pale. Something so newly dead should not be so withered, should it?

Registering Krýl's aversion to the mound of carrion the symbiote reacted. A moment later and the eukaryotic shell had him locked away, shredding his tunic and trousers in the process. He tugged the remains of his borrowed clothing from his shoulders and let the rags fall.

For a long while Krýl stood and stared at the pod. At last he took several squelching steps forward and lifted away its top with one clawed hand. The pod split with a wet crack, drooling long strands of mucus. Tossing the cover aside, Krýl looked down at the figure nestled within.

The slack features of the corpse were familiar. Not long ago that face had been beset with worry. It had implored him to find a lost girl, one that had been taken in the night. He had found the child, or what remained of her. Now the woman lay inside one of the Witch's pods, her own flesh sallow and wasted.

"Trespass!"

The sudden cry came from above, a reedy accusation that cut through Krýl's reverie and sent a bolt of panic up his spine. He jerked his head up towards the rectangle of light that seemed to hover overhead. Outlined against this brighter patch was the silhouette of a man. Instinctively, Krýl raised the lighted tendrils towards the opening. Before he could catch a glimpse of the figure's face it swung up into the room above and the portal clattered shut.

WRATH

——•●•——

One

Krýl could feel his heartbeat in his temples and sweat on his palms. The armor lapped at the moisture, tasting the salt, the traces of sugar and ammonia. His gaze swept the chamber, searching the shadows, the rotten bulk of the carnal heap. At last his eye came back to the outline of the hatch set in the ceiling. Through the seams around its edges he could see movement. Straining his ears he caught the hint of voices speaking in low tones.

Taking a deep breath Krýl forced himself towards calm. Shaking his head, he sneered at his own cowardice. Were it not for the sense of dread he had cultivated at the sight of this place, this dumping ground, he would never have reacted so. He was a soldier, after all. A few bloated white snails shouldn't be cause for alarm. Then again, beyond all the death and decay, there was the Witch.

He was an interloper in her exclusive world of plants, of insects, of whatever it was that lay within the pod half buried in the pile of corpses. She would not be pleased, this redoubtable yet capricious woman. She was proud and cruel, possessed of an ego nearly as large as her intellect. Should she feel in the least bit slighted, Krýl had no doubt he would bear the brunt of her wrath.

For a moment he contemplated bursting through the hatch, killing whomever or whatever was on the other side. This, however, would require an external source of food lest the armor use him to power its own growth. Under normal conditions the pile of corpses at his feet would be more than adequate. But not these. Never these. The armor found them nearly as repulsive as he did.

Spitting invectives Krýl turned around and kicked at the slime and decay. One of the white snails went flying, striking the far wall and splitting open. The sound made him cringe.

Krýl shook his head, disgusted at his own lack of foresight as much as the heap of bones. He had allowed himself to be taken by surprise, to be locked in this underground chamber of horrors. If only he hadn't let his need to know get the better of him.

Krýl drew back his foot for another kick, then hesitated.

No, this little expedition hadn't been because of a compulsion on his part. It had been the Shade's idea. That insubstantial wisp of sentient shadow had prodded him towards whatever it was the Witch kept locked away in her greenhouses. Had it not been for the cry he had heard in the garden and the Shade's subsequent goading, he never would have come.

Beneath the carapace Krýl's brow furrowed and his lip twitched.

Why would an ancient ghost, a thing that was only half

alive, care whether there were screams in the night? Why would it drive him to satisfy his own curiosity on the subject? Krýl hadn't the slightest idea. The more he thought about it, the less it made sense. The less sense it made the more agitated he became.

"Calm."

Krýl rolled his head from side to side, listening to his vertebra crackle and pop. Working himself into a frenzy would accomplish nothing. He would ask the Shade a few choice questions later. For now...

Raising the cluster of glowing filaments, Krýl passed it around the chamber. He watched as the wan blue light glinted off bones, snails, and flesh. The light came to rest on the pod that dominated the heap of carrion.

Focusing on the woman tucked inside, Krýl took a step forward. There was a quality to her, something beyond his having known her in life.

Krýl took another step, sinking to his calf in slime. He ignored it, taking another step, and then another. Soon he was compelled to go to all fours. The armor cringed, urged him to move back, to cease contact. He pushed on. When he was again standing beside the pod he lowered the glowing bundle of filaments, bathing the corpse in blue light.

The woman had been a fool. The fat man as well. They had allowed the child in their care to be taken, snatched from under their noses. The girl had been intended for the Witch, a rare specimen purchased through agents months in advance. The woman in the pod had lost her to wormrotters.

Had this been her punishment, to be cocooned alive? No, that seemed unlikely. The Witch had hanged her companion from her battlements with his guts around his ankles. Had she simply wanted to punish the woman the Witch could have done any number of things. But this...this was something else entirely.

Krýl brought the light closer then suddenly drew it back again. A jolt ran through him and he nearly fell from the heap of carrion. Willing the membranes covering his eyes to pull back he again bent over the dead woman. He traced the lines of her flesh, pressing the light closer still.

No, this was not punishment.

The skin which Krýl had at first taken to be pale even for a corpse was, in fact, nearly translucent. Through the woman's skin could be seen muscles and tendons interlaced with a web of blood vessels. Though her angular features and thin carriage were a far cry from the Witch's curves, this corpse was an unmistakable doppelganger—a partially finished copy of the Pellucid Witch herself.

From above there came a thud and the sound of tromping feet. Krýl raised his head, the transparent membranes he had pulled back again sliding over his eyes. He moved from the heap of corpses, snails falling to either side, and put his back to the wall. Again he cursed himself for lingering. He should have slid a tendril around the latch and charged whoever was waiting for him above.

The trap door fell aside with a bang. The membranes over Krýl's eyes darkened, filtering the light from above. Unconsciously, he extended a single, jagged length of chitin from his right wrist, feeling a pang in his chest as the armor siphoned his base components to feed its growth.

"Krýl."

The Witch's voice was flat and cold. On her lips the sound of his name seemed like an admonishment.

"Come out."

Krýl waited, gazing up into the square hole in the ceiling. Beyond his hostess he could see nothing but the glare of energy bulbs.

"I said come out!"

There was a clank and rustle as unseen soldiers shifted their position. They were nervous. Krýl knew as much even if the armor hadn't been able to smell their fear. They were expectant, taut as bowstrings. He would make them wait. As their tension grew so did his advantage.

Krýl began to count. He reached twenty seconds, then thirty. At forty he moved.

Tendrils burst from between Krýl's shoulders. They shot upwards, barbed ends grasping the edges of the hole. With a sudden rush the armor retracted the tendrils, pulling him up and into the light. Balancing on the writhing filaments he took several steps in reverse until his back struck solid rock.

From both left and right came the sound of safety catches being flicked from crossbows. Two more tentacles extended themselves from Krýl's back. Tipped with serrated lengths of chitin they cut at the air, waving themselves back and forth.

The Witch laughed. She put one delicate hand to her lips and shook her head. "Those won't help you."

Krýl glanced about this, the largest of the Witch's many greenhouses. Spread out before him were a dozen guards, crossbows leveled. At their sides hung scimitars and long knives, on their heads were steel helmets.

Now it was Krýl's turn to laugh.

"I cut a swathe through your cavalry the day we met. What chance do you think these men have?"

The Witched waved his scorn away. "You gave a good enough account of yourself. In fact you killed several of my finest. This is why I invited you to my home. This is why I deigned to show you my collections." Here she paused and examined the fingernails of her right hand. "It was in one of these collections, in the menagerie, that you saw the small blue and yellow frogs."

Puzzled, Krýl shifted to one side. The tendrils that extended from his back quavered, twitched.

"I believe," said the Witch, "that I informed you of the purpose to which I put the poison the frogs secrete?"

Krýl's heart went cold. Beneath the insulating layers of armor he felt his skin prickle. For its part the eukaryotic shell seemed to register the threat, sending a warning directly into the back of his brain.

"My men apply the toxin to their daggers," said the Witch, "and to the bolts of their crossbows."

Slowly Krýl withdrew the blade that had extended itself from his wrist. This was followed by the serrated tentacles. A few seconds later and he had lowered himself to the floor. Once again standing on his own two feet he spread his hands to the sides, palms up.

"Good," said the Witch. "Now get on your knees."

Krýl did not move.

"Your knees," hissed the Witch.

"No," said Krýl.

"Last chance."

Krýl raised his chin. "No."

The Witch twitched a finger and two crossbows loosed their bolts. These were followed a split second later by two more. Krýl twisted between the first pair of the missiles, tendrils knocking them aside. The second pair caught him in the side and thigh. He felt them go in, felt the armor close around them, arresting their progress before they could penetrate his flesh.

Krýl felt the eukaryotic shell force a geyser of adrenaline into his system.

The Witch bared her teeth in an animal grin.

He had underestimated her wrath. The Witch was

unafraid, willing to sacrifice her men and property in order to wreak bloody vengeance upon his trespass.

Forming the tips of the remaining tendrils into jagged barbs, Krýl whipped them to both left and right. The first two crossbowmen screamed as their arms and weapons clattered to the stones.

Sweeping the tendrils back and forth like scythes, Krýl charged. Men fell away clutching bloodied stumps, grasping at opened throats and bellies. Offal and crimson struck the floor, thrown about like so many castoffs from an abattoir. Two more men died, then three, then five.

The Witch, her head high, took a few measured steps back. Around her blood settled on the leaves of the surrounding flora, pattering down like spring rain.

As more guardsmen filed in around her, Krýl heard the Witch speak, her voice cutting through the din as clear as crystal. "Silver and rubies," she said. "Silver and rubies for the man who brings him down."

Bolts struck Krýl in the sides, in the arms, the legs, the chest. He felt them bore into the armor, felt the fungoid shell harden around their tips then spit them out.

Another breathless second elapsed; another four men died. The armor ensnared one of the newly minted corpses, dragging it in Krýl's wake, siphoning off blood, flesh, and marrow.

Taking the edge of a scimitar on his forearms, Krýl turned the blade then rammed his fist into the face of the man behind it. The man fell away spitting blood and teeth. The next guardsman in line died under the armor's lashing tentacles, his heart pierced through.

Krýl kicked the body free then broke into a run, eyes fixed on the Witch. He took three bounding leaps, then collapsed in a heap on the greenhouse floor. His head struck the stones, stars dancing before his eyes.

"Enough!"

The Witch's command thrummed like a gong. Krýl felt the knell as much as heard it. In response the rain of quarrels ceased.

Krýl raised himself to his knees, his chin lolling on his chest. Around him the armor felt heavy, unresponsive. To either side the tendrils hung limp, stretched out across the blood-spattered floor like barbed creepers. His breath came thick and heavy, the gill slits on either side of his helmet dripping with mucus. He tried to rise, tried to force the armor to heave itself up, to lash out at the approaching figure. It would not move.

The Witch took several steps forward, bent down and lifted Krýl's chin with one finger. "Gauche," she said. "Gauche and uninspired."

Krýl tried to pull his head away, but the Witch grasped his chin and dug in her nails.

"I offered you hospitality. I offered you my bed. You chose to violate the sanctity of my greenhouses. You went sifting through nearly every room, nearly every carefully controlled environment. In doing so you contaminated everything."

Krýl again tried to rise, tried to speak. His lips moved, but no sound came out. Glancing to the side he saw that where the quarrels had imbedded themselves in the armor its surface was blackened. Even as he watched it began to slough and peel. It fell away like ashes, bits of shell disintegrating even as they struck the floor.

"Foolish," said the Witch, letting Krýl's chin drop and taking a step back. "Foolish, to challenge me, to spit in my face."

Krýl's head lolled drunkenly.

"What I at first took to be courage on your part was nothing but stupidity. You are not a warrior. You are nothing but a dog, a cur fit only to grovel and beg for scraps beneath my table."

She kicked him then, planting one foot in the middle of his chest and sending him sprawling. This time when Krýl's head hit the floor he saw nothing but darkness.

Two

Of all the men and women Krýl had encountered, had broken bread or spilled blood with, the Witch was unique. He had known warlords that could not be surfeited even after they had gorged themselves on bloodshed. He had known merchants continuously seeking profit though their coffers were full. The Witch was just as covetous, yet she alone seemed to possess a sense of perspective. This was evident in the time and care spent shaping her keep, her gardens, her collections.

The warlords and merchants Krýl had known were small men, bandits and profiteers that had carved out a niche for themselves only to overreach and tumble back into obscurity. For a chance at seizing the accumulated wealth of the Pellucid Witch, Krýl knew they would have slain each other to a man. Perhaps not so long ago he would have joined them. Much had changed since his coming to this place.

Though the Witch was as sybaritic as the warlords and merchants, unlike them her calculating self-interest and relative isolation had allowed her to rise to prominence without the threat of competition. She was like a lýr-cat that has wandered from its traditional hunting grounds and found itself alone in a virgin wilderness. Far from civilization, further still from the petty squabbles of landed nobles, warlords, or nomads, the Witch had no need to fight over the same tracts of bloodied earth that passed endlessly back and forth. She was free to do as she pleased. Here, in this secluded valley, she could tend her gardens and rule as she saw fit. Even so, this did nothing to mitigate her cruelty. And, just like a lýr-cat, she would follow a grudge to the ends of the earth.

Krýl watched her turn, the muscles beneath her skin tensing and relaxing, visible through skin as limpid as blown glass. The Witch adjusted something on a panel, a solid sheet of curving and etched porcelain punctuated by small dials and levers. Through bleary eyes he followed the graceful movement of her hands as they traced the contours of the console. Like everything else in the Witch's keep it was unique, a marvel of the Old World, a thing of surpassing beauty preserved by this remarkable woman. What purpose it served he could not begin to guess.

The Witch stepped to another panel, her fingers gently brushing a series of switches. Tiny lights flickered on, bright in the dim glow that lit the small, tidy room. Somewhere behind him, Krýl heard a machine whir to life. The whir grew then faded into an insectoid buzzing that filled his head and set his teeth on edge.

Stepping towards him, the Witch raised one hand and drew down on something suspended above Krýl's head. He heard steel sliding over steel. A moment later and there was a sharp pain in his shoulder. This was followed by another, and then another. The Witch continued to jab him, moving down the line of his spine inch by inch. Krýl raised his head. The Witch stopped what she was doing and straightened. "No," she said softly, "do not move."

She pushed Krýl's head back down then returned to jabbing him. Moving to his waist she punctured the skin at the small of his back a half dozen more times.

As his eyes continued to come in and out of focus, Krýl peered at his own reflection in the polished marble of the floor. He tried to make sense of what he saw. Held in place by a steel armature, the rack on which he was hung fit snuggly around his arms and legs, neck and torso. Over this frame loomed a mechanical arm, an elegant instrument made of gleaming metal. At its end was threaded a collection of wires. In the soft glow of the overhead spheres the wires shimmered like strands of spider silk.

Krýl's breath caught in his throat. The wires protruded from where the eukaryotic shell had retreated after the Witch's touch had driven it back.

Moving around to the front of the frame, the Witch again took Krýl's head in her hands. He tried to pull away, but she held him in place. It did not take much effort. The poison that had leached into his system through the armor had utterly drained him. He felt like an infant, aware of his own body, but unable to make it respond.

"Nearly finished," said the Witch. Her voice was calm, almost soothing.

A shiver ran up Krýl's spine and his arms and legs broke out in gooseflesh. Seeing this, the corners of the Witch's lips turned up in a humorless little smile.

Reaching behind his head she drew forth another of the tiny needles and its accompanying thread. This she inserted into the back of Krýl's neck.

The Witch ran cold fingers along the back of his head. "Remain still. The next needle I insert will be directly into your spine. Twist but a fraction of an inch to either side and you may find yourself paralyzed, or perhaps unable to breathe." Then, with aching slowness, she slipped the needle between his vertebrae.

"There," said the Witch, "one more and that will be the

last of them." Her voice came to Krýl as an echo, a low susur-rus that bypassed his ears and caressed the surface of his mind. A moment later and he felt her fingers at the nape of his neck. "Each of the needles has been inserted into a major nerve or cluster of nerves. They are a part of you now, just as much as the symbiote. To disrupt them would be…unfortu-nate. That being said, this will be very, very painful."

Fire lanced through the base of Krýl's skull. For an instant his vision went blank. The burning sensation in his skull increased, threatening to burst from his mouth, his nose, his eyes. He gritted his teeth, felt the needles in his spine shift, and forced himself to relax.

"Finished," said the Witch.

Krýl whimpered.

The Witched laughed.

"I can hear you now," she said, "your thoughts, your emotions. Before, the symbiote kept me at bay. Now that it has gone dormant I have free rein. I can slip behind your eyes and pry from you whatever information I desire."

Krýl felt his heart skip a beat. The thought that the Witch could burrow into his mind was disturbing, yes, but it was nothing compared to the knowledge that the symbiote was no longer at his beck and call. It had been reduced to little more than a fungal infection, unwilling or unable to do more than simply exist.

The Witch leaned closer, her lips nearly brushing Krýl's ear. "I do not have to dig very deep to know that you are far less interesting than even I suspected. It is true that you are slightly more perceptive than the average soldier, but like every fighting man I have ever known you live for duty, and duty alone. The only difference between you and the others is that you have no nation to which you can pledge your loy-alty. You are a wanderer, a vagrant. More pathetic still, your ambitions run along such banal lines as your next meal, your next job, your next chance to rut. Truly, you are little more than an animal."

Krýl recoiled as though he had been slapped. He felt his face go red. The Witch tittered.

"Poor dear, I seem to have hit a nerve." This brought another tinkling little laugh. "Now stay still, do not strain against the needles."

The thought of straining at his bonds, of ripping his hands free and clamping them around the Witch's throat rose to the forefront of Krýl's mind. The Witch saw as much. "Mongrel!" she hissed. "You wouldn't dare."

Despite the ice in her tone Krýl's rage redoubled. He tensed the muscles of his arms and shoulders, pulled against the straps that held his wrists. The resulting pain in his neck and back nearly drove him to unconsciousness. With a whimper Krýl let himself go limp.

The Witch snorted. "Despite your impudence—your boorishness—you have one trait that I admire." She paused, put a finger to her lips. "No, make that two. Though your curiosity has been your downfall I would count it a virtue. I myself would not be where I am today if it were not for my insatiable desire to learn more, always more. Secondly, you seem just as stubborn, as unwilling to surrender, as I am. But unlike you, this stubbornness extends to my own mortality."

Krýl tensed, immediately regretting the sudden movement.

The Witch's smile returned. "I have lived more lifetimes than you could possibly imagine. Do you think a fortress like mine, a collection like mine, a garden like mine can be so quickly and easily obtained that one lifetime would suffice? I refuse to let my mind perish with a single body."

An image of the carnal heap, the pod, and the body

within filled Krýl's mind.

"Exactly," said the Witch. "The child I purchased, the one that foolish woman and her fat friend lost, was special, gifted. She was more than a means to an end. Her body would have provided me with talents beyond anything you could possibly imagine." Here she trailed off and raised her eyes to the ceiling. "A momentary lapse and she was gone."

She had been so small, had weighed almost nothing. Krýl did his best to push the memory aside.

The Witch lowered her eyes. "You, at least, made an effort to win her back. You at least tried to save her life. Had you succeeded I would have made you a prince. Such a pity that it has come down to this."

Krýl peered up at the Witch. He could see her more clearly now, the blurriness momentarily having faded to the periphery of his vision.

"The world is old," she said, "the sun is old. What were once individual continents have drifted, fused into one. The planet is unbalanced. "

Krýl gasped as images flooded his mind. Drawn directly from the Witch's own memories they cascaded over his consciousness like a river tumbling over jagged rocks. He was carried along with the current, helpless to do aught but watch.

"Our vast, single ocean absorbs too much of the sun's energy. It drinks it in then releases it upon this last great continent. Our bloated red sun has burned the land, etched the rocks in its own bloody image. Here, in the interior, the crystalline storms grow in duration and intensity. They scour whole forests, whole cities."

A string of drool seeped from between Krýl's lips. He felt it slip down, down to the floor.

"In my many lifetimes I have seen whole cultures rise and fall. I have watched as religions have been spawned, grown bloated and opulent, then faded away to nothing. Humanity has changed dozens of times, adapting, our ever-changing genes carrying us further and further apart. The different subspecies war with one another, each vying for supremacy. Soon true humanity may cease to exist entirely."

Krýl's vision returned as his mind's eye went blank.

The Witch lowered her head and wrapped her arms around her middle. When she looked up again her eyes were as hard and cold as iron.

"The oceans are dying. The land is dying. But I refuse to die with them. I will live on even if that means subsuming every man, woman, and child."

A long silence followed, punctuated only by the gentle whir and buzz of the Witch's machines. At last Krýl found his voice. It croaked from his throat like the wind from the desert. "And what of me?"

The Witch's demeanor softened and she smiled. She reached out one delicate hand and touched his bald scalp. "I am going to pry the symbiote from you. I will rip it out by the roots if that's what it takes."

The image of the Witch faded, replaced by that of the lýr-cat.

"Unlike you, the shell is unique. It has survived; it has adapted. You do not deserve such a gift. We have much in common, this shell and I. So I will take it."

Krýl choked out a single, "No."

The Witch patted his head. "You have some inkling of what this means," she said. "Good."

And Krýl did. With the symbiote gone he would be little more than an empty vessel, a thing only half alive.

Straightening her gown the Witch strode to a panel set in the far wall. Here she adjusted one dial then another, waiting until a series of tiny lights were illuminated. When this was done she turned and peered over her shoulder. "Almost ready."

Krýl's guts squirmed themselves into a knot.

The Witch flicked one, two, three switches. She hesitated before flicking the fourth. "I dearly wish you had been more interesting."

The click of the last switch seemed to reverberate throughout the whole of time and space. That single sharp note was elongated, lifted, spread across the cosmos. It hung about Krýl like a pall, droning and looping back upon itself. He felt his mouth open, felt the scream that came tumbling from his lips, but heard nothing save the reverberating knell of the switch.

Fire danced across his nerve endings. It seared his flesh from within, a conflagration that neither consumed nor blackened, but burned nonetheless. Each fiber of his being, each atom was set alight. The flames tugged at him, pulled him this way and that. Krýl felt as though he were being segmented, butchered at the most basic level of existence. Then, the first of the fibrils came lose.

It was as if part of him had broken away and gone drifting through the ether. A vacuum appeared where once there had been consciousness, a living presence in sync with his own. When the second fibril was torn away the feeling redoubled and the void grew. Everything that Krýl was, everything he had been, reeled. Emptiness yawned before him, utterly devoid of sense, of thought, of existence. Krýl felt as though he would fall, swallowed by the void, doomed to plummet for eternity.

Amidst this growing sense of unreality, he felt the presence of the eukaryotic shell. As each fibril was ripped free it came slowly out of its stupor. Krýl felt it mirror his own desperation, felt it strive desperately to remain a part of him.

A silent scream, as deep and as anguished as the void, filled his head. The scream cut through the burning sensation that agonized his every nerve, howling at the effrontery of being pulled from its host. Krýl latched on to that sense of injustice, that feeling of being wronged even as he was torn apart.

The Witch was old, the Witch was clever, the Witch was heir to learning and technology the likes of which Krýl could barely fathom. Through them she had removed herself from the world, detaching herself from its natural processes. She had cheated death itself. But for all of her knowledge and her experience, she was isolated, alone, cut off from her environment.

The eukaryotic shell, that ancient primordial thing, had lived a millennia before the Witch had first drawn breath. It was instinct and ferocity, an insatiable drive to consume, to adapt, to live. Against these base tenants of life how could all the art and science of a bygone age hope to stand? While the empires that had birthed the Witch's machines crumbled, the eukaryotic shell had lived on. It had adapted; it had persevered. And Krýl, was he not a part of that same organism?

His right arm was the first to come free, drenched in sweat, the wrist cut and bleeding. Metal struck the floor of the laboratory, the shattered restraint skittering away across its mirrored surface.

At the sound of the shackle striking the tiles the Witch spun, her robe swirling about her hips and shoulders like storm-tossed clouds. Before her hung Krýl, his head lowered, his naked arms and legs a mass of knotted muscle. Sweat beaded his forehead, ran down his cheeks, dripped from his nose and chin. As she watched, the needles in his neck and spine began to come loose. One by one they were expelled from Krýl's flesh, to hang suspended on their shimmering wires.

The Witch started forward, one hand outstretched.

Krýl pulled against the restraint holding his left wrist in place, grinding at the metal until blood ran down his arm.

The Witch's hand struck the control panel beside him, and she manically began flipping switches and turn dials.

With another metallic crack the second coffle came loose. The Witch jumped at the sound, and she flung a look of panic in Krýl's direction. An instant later and her features had hardened.

"No!"

The Witch slammed down on a level and warning bells began to sound.

"NO!"

Krýl pulled his left ankle free and reached for the bar across his chest.

RECKONING

————•●•————

One

Flames spilled from the door of the laboratory, greedy orange tongues that moved along the walls and the ceiling, lapping at the stonework. Smoke rolled the length and breadth of the corridor, turning the air into a scorching miasma. The orbs that lined the hall winked out as the heat reached them, popping like lýthipods beneath a boot.

Silhouetted against the holocaust glow that roared from the laboratory Krýl stood hunched, one hand propped against the wall. Soot clung to the jagged surface of the symbiote, streaking it black. Reflected firelight danced across the membranes that covered his eyes, turning them into glowing embers. From his wrists grew chitinous extrusions, their edges broken and serrated. Large patches of the armored shell, still the victim of the Witch's poison, were flaked and peeling. Even so, the guardsmen that packed into the corridor quailed, shook, inched themselves backwards.

Krýl did not speak, did not roar, did not charge. He simply put one foot in front of the other. Stumbling, his hand trailing along the wall, he let the armor dictate his movements. The guardsmen continued to shuffle backwards, their eyes wide, their knuckles white on the hilts of their swords. By the time the first of them had regained enough of his wits to turn and run Krýl was on them.

They fell to broad, sweeping strokes, limbs cut away, their throats opened. Krýl lingered for a moment, letting the armor siphon off as much blood as it could before the flames at his back drove him forward.

As he forced himself down the corridor, Krýl spared a solitary glance to his rear. The flames that spilled from the laboratory door had grown in size and intensity. As he watched they swallowed the guardsmen, immersing them in a puddle of molten stone. Krýl wondered for a moment at what manner of chemicals the Witch had kept in her sanctum sanctorum, what manner of fire could melt stone.

A sudden gout of flame followed by a booming report filled the corridor. Krýl was driven back against the wall, his feet going out from under him. He put his hands over his face as a great cloud of smoke and soot went reeling by. When it had cleared he pulled himself upright, used his hands as guides, and made his way from the inferno.

The deviant woman stood with her hands against the glass partition. Her head moved from side to side, her tongue flicking from her lipless mouth. On her face and in her sightless pink eyes was an expression of dread. Upon seeing her Krýl drew up short.

How had he found his way to her enclosure? He did not know. Since dragging himself from the burning laboratory

Krýl had been aware only of stumbling from one corridor to the next. With each step the eukaryotic shell had grown stronger while he had grown weaker, more delirious. Aside from the nutrients siphoned from the slaughtered guardsmen the shell had had nothing with which to sustain itself. This meant the armor had turned on him, consuming his body to feed its own. Now he stood before the Witch's pet deviant, wracked with fatigue, his mind reduced to a jumble of images, emotions, and imperatives. Escape and food, these were the only things that mattered. Yet here he was, the blind albino flicking her tongue at him.

Krýl took another step forward.

The deviant woman again tasted the air. She raised her head, turned sightless pink eyes towards where he stood swaying. "You," she said softly.

Krýl teetered, caught himself against the doorframe. He looked down at his legs, his torso. Already the dark patches along his sides had begun to shrink as the armor slowly expelled the Witch's poison. Still it needed more... more flesh, more blood, more bone.

"I taste flame," said the deviant woman. "I taste ash."

Staggering forward Krýl fell against the glass partition. It shuddered, but did not break. He slumped against its smooth surface, his clawed fingers splayed. Through the fogged membranes that covered his eyes he saw the deviant woman shudder.

"What did she do to you?"

Krýl could not respond, could only rake his talons down the partition. They scored the glass, leaving a trail of shallow furrows. The deviant woman took a step back.

"Krýl...what have you done?"

Krýl's talons dug a second row of furrows in the glass.

"Krýl?"

The armor opened vents along Krýl's neck and lower jaw. It tasted the air just as the deviant woman had done. It smelled her fear, smelled the blood that rushed just below the surface of her pearlescent scales.

"Listen to me, Krýl. Listen to my voice."

"Aílea."

"Yes, Aílea! And you…you are Krýl."

Aílea's words went echoing through his skull, knocking about like a wooden ball thrown into an empty room.

The armor drew another deep breath and flooded Krýl's brain with dopamine and endorphins. It urged him to curl his hand into a fist and strike at the glass.

"Krýl?" Aílea stepped forward and placed her palm to the glass opposite his own. "Krýl, speak to me."

She was beautiful, her scales reflecting the sunlight from the high set windows of her enclosure. She was like a living jewel, an opal in the guise of a woman.

Krýl struck the glass with one barbed fist.

Aílea took a quick step back.

Krýl struck the glass again and a thin spider web of cracks appeared.

She was breathing heavily now, one hand to her breast. Krýl could smell cortisol and adrenaline. The armor urged him to strike the glass again.

Aílea took another step back, her tongue darting in and out of her mouth, her blind eyes darting to left and right.

Krýl hit the glass a third time. More cracks appeared.

The symbiote cried out for flesh, for blood, for bone. It cried out for the Witch's favorite plaything, for the opalescent creature that stood just on the other side of the glass partition.

When the Witch had tired of her she had been locked away, reduced to a curio. Krýl would not leave her by the wayside, would not forget about her. He would strip away her shimmering flesh, let the armor take her inside of itself.

"My name," said the deviant woman, her voice barely above a whisper, "is Aílea. Your name is Krýl."

Krýl struck the glass, and struck the glass, and struck the glass. The spider web of cracks grew larger, tiny splinters of glass falling from his knuckles to the floor.

"Aílea," breathed the deviant woman, tears welling in her eyes. "My name is Aílea!"

She had retreated nearly to the back of the enclosure. Beneath slanting rays of sunlight her scales winked and sparkled like stars. Krýl watched her flesh glow, watched the light play off of her shoulders, her breasts, her hips.

"My name…"

Krýl gave the barrier one final vicious blow, shattering it. A hundred thousand razor keen shards fell to the floor in a glittering arch. Krýl stood at their center, shoulders hunched, arms dangling at his sides.

Aílea sank to the ground and tucked her knees up to her chest. She put her head down, closed her eyes, and waited.

The crossbow bolt took Krýl in the shoulder. It bit through the still fragile shell of the symbiote, burying itself in flesh and scraping bone. Krýl, half-turned by the impact, went to one knee. Twisting his head around he saw a cadre of guardsmen, one of them already bending to wind the mechanism on his crossbow.

"Now! Take him!"

There was a pause as the soldiers looked to one another, each waiting for his fellow to be the first into the breach. Krýl filled the dead space with whirling death.

Heedless of the bolt protruding from his shoulder, Krýl barreled into the guardsmen. They had piled themselves atop the stairs leading to Aílea's enclosure, an off-balance jumble of men and armor unable to turn or maneuver. The force of his charge drove them backwards. Together they went tumbling down the stairs, their crashing like thunder against the stone. And as they fell Krýl hewed and cut, butchering his way through one soldier then the next. Where his blade met flesh, the symbiote fed. By the time the hurtling pile of men and weapons crashed to the bottom of the stairs the armor had given Krýl back to himself.

There he lay, staring at the floor, listening to the wet sounds of meat being pulled from bone. Krýl shut his eyes and drew a deep breath.

To his left one of the guardsmen began to pray. Krýl opened his eyes and turned towards the figure. Holding his entrails in place with both hands the guardsman looked off into space and chanted his litany. Krýl listened for a moment. He did not recognize the words. Whatever the man's faith it was foreign to him.

Krýl got to his feet, shuffled to where the guardsman lay, and grasped him by the collar. Feeling the nearness of the wounded man the symbiote extended delicate tendrils towards the pile of intestines in the man's lap.

"The Witch, where would she go...where would she go if she had been injured?"

The wounded man jerked as the tendrils began to work. Krýl recognized him as one of the men that had watched him work at the straw dummies in the practice yard.

"Where would she go?"

The wounded man began to pray even louder.

"Where is she? Where would she go to die?" Krýl's words echoed from the stone walls.

From below there came a wet, slurping noise and the guardsman went limp.

Krýl dropped the body and turned back towards the

stairs. Around him lay a heap of carrion. Looking up the spiral of steps he saw that the ceiling, the walls, the stairs were stained red. Cruor dripped from the tiles overhead, ran in rivulets between the ancient stones.

Aílea screamed.

Yanking free the feeding tendrils Krýl bolted up the stairs. He took them three at a time, bursting into the enclosure.

Aílea sat where he had left her, huddled in a ball. Krýl took several steps towards her, glass crunching beneath his feet. A twinge in his shoulder made him stop. He waited as the armor expelled the crossbow bolt from his flesh, the missile falling to the flagging with a clatter.

"Blood and fire."

Krýl turned his head to one side.

"So much blood and fire!"

Krýl moved into the enclosure. Slowly he bent down and bundled Aílea into his arms. As he pressed her to his chest he heard her sob once, then fall silent.

Two

In what remained of the nymph's enclosure there lingered a scent like boiled fish. Through the blackened glass Krýl could see three of them rolling and bobbing as their grotto bubbled and seethed. The air was filled with condensation, every surface wet and dripping. The eukaryotic shell opened vents along Krýl's sides, soaking up the moisture.

Aílea made a distressed noise, something between a gasp and a hiss. "What…what do you see?"

Face down and arms outstretched the nymphs rolled and bobbed.

"Nothing," said Krýl. "It's too dark."

"You're lying. Tell me what you see."

The body of one of the nymphs sank, reappeared, moved towards the glass. It struck the barrier with a dull thud. The flesh along its side broke, the meat sloughing from the bone beneath. Hungrily the symbiote reached for it. Krýl forced the feeding tendrils back.

"Tell me …"

"The glass is blacked and the energy bulbs have all burned out. The only light is from the far wall. The fire's heated the stones, boiled the pool."

Aílea put a hand to her mouth.

Krýl squinted into the dimness, watched the stones along the far wall wink like embers. The glow increased and a thin rivulet of molten stone detached itself from the wall and slid languidly into the pool.

"The fire's eating through the wall. We need to go."

Aílea opened her mouth and began to pant. "I can feel the heat of it, like the sun at midday. Is this your doing, did you start the fire?"

Krýl ignored the question. "The last I saw of the Witch she was injured, burned. Before I could reach her she disappeared behind a wall of smoke. We need to find her. I need to find her."

Aílea turned her face towards Krýl, nictitating membranes sliding over her sightless eyes. "What did she do to you that you would cause so much destruction?" She paused, looked towards the bubbling pool, then back at Krýl. "It does not matter, not anymore. You are free; you are yourself again."

"I need to find her."

"We need to help the others."

"Others?"

Aílea gestured towards the door with her chin. "The crystal man, the nymphs…"

"The nymphs are dead. In another few minutes—"

A shape struck the blackened glass with enough force to set the partition to vibrating. Aílea screamed. Krýl raised one bladed fist, then slowly lowered it. The nymph that pressed herself against the glass looked like a corpse that did not have enough sense to lie down. Most of her body was blistered and torn. Her cheeks were gone, exposing the needle-like teeth beneath. Both eyes had turned white, the retinas dethatched, the lids boiled away. Her hair, what remained of it, hung limp and in patches.

Once, twice, the nymph beat a webbed hand against the glass. Even when her palm split she continued to strike the partition. Where she struck the glass she left bloodied hand prints, one overlapping the other.

"We need to go," said Krýl.

It did not seem bothered by the heat. Krýl envied the creature, huddled beside a waterfall of molten stone, seemingly inured to the impending destruction all around it. He watched as the burning wall hissed and spat, a glob of molten stone landing on its shoulder. The crystalline deviant brushed it away, then returned to sitting and staring at the floor.

"It's not going to move," said Krýl. "Plead with it all you like, it seems content to stay and to die."

"Come," said Aílea, her hand outstretched. "Please."

The crystalline deviant remained where he was.

"Come," said Aílea. "You must come! If you do not, the keep will burn down around you!"

The crystalline deviant turned its head slowly, fixing her with golden eyes. Aílea moved closer, her outstretched hand groping. When she reached the creature she touched its shoulder with delicate fingers. It did not balk or withdraw, simply continued to stare, its gaze intent on Aílea.

"We've run out of time," said Krýl. "The walls have

started to buckle."

On all sides the stonework was misshapen, the ceiling bowed. Even within the eukaryotic shell he could feel the heat, like the inside of a forge. He wondered how Aílea was still standing.

"Please…" Aílea moved her hand from the creature's shoulder and gently brushed its cheek. "You will die…"

"Perhaps," said Krýl. "Perhaps not. He's from the wastes. He's more crystal than man."

Aílea put down her head, her chin to her chest. "Even he could not survive flames hot enough to melt stone."

"And neither can we."

Taking the deviant woman by the shoulder, Krýl dragged her towards the open door. Aílea resisted, pushing at his hand, struggling to return to the crystalline deviant.

"No! If we leave him…"

"If we leave him, he'll have as much of a chance as we do. Now stop squirming!"

Aílea slapped Krýl's hand away. With tears in her eyes she leveled an accusatory finger at his chest. "You, who have killed so many, who has set this whole keep ablaze—you do not get a say in this matter! Either he comes with us, or I stay with him."

Krýl felt his jaw clench, felt the armor ripple. He leveled a finger of his own, then tucked it back into his fist.

The crystalline deviant had moved from beside the cascade of molten stone. It had matched their steps, moving in the direction they had, moving towards the open door. "Stop being so bloody dramatic. If we lead, it will follow."

Aílea raised her head and tested the air with her tongue.

"He's right behind you."

Putting out a hand the blind deviant groped for the creature. When her fingers brushed its pate she smiled.

"Come," said Krýl.

Aílea wiped at her cheeks. There was no need, her tears had burned away before they could fall.

Three

The primates shrieked, bounded from limb to limb, scrabbling over the dead tree that filled their enclosure. They could smell the smoke, the ash that drifted on the hot air. Instinct told them to flee, but flee they could not. Instead they scampered along the dead wood, swinging from their gilded cage, beating themselves against the bars. Several of the smaller ones lay dead at the bottom of the enclosure, their fur matted and filthy.

Aílea stood at the base of the cage gazing sightlessly up at the latticework of iron. The primates in turn shrieked their fear and frustration down at her.

"Release them."

Krýl looked down at Aílea, then back up at the primates.

"Release them."

"Stay or go, they're dead either way. The keep is burning, soon the gardens will be as well. Beyond this place there's only desert."

"Set them free," said Aílea. "Allow them a chance to live. Do not condemn them to die like the nymphs."

Krýl shuddered; the armor salivated.

From beside him there came the sound of stone grating on stone. Krýl looked down to see the crystalline deviant moving in the direction of the cage. The creature's steps were slow and deliberate, unhurried even as the keep burned down around its head.

"Please…"

Krýl turned back to the deviant woman. "The Witch is still out there somewhere. Let her deal with them."

When the crystalline deviant reached the door to the primate's enclosure it raised one gnarled hand to the lock. It wrapped its fist around the mechanism and squeezed. The metal gave. The deviant then turned and made its way back towards Krýl and Aílea. Behind it the door swung open, its hinges squealing.

"Are they…have they fled?"

"No. They're just sitting there looking foolish."

The crystalline deviant drew up beside them and sat as immobile and silent as stone.

Aílea opened her mouth to speak, but instead began to cough. Smoke lay thick in the menagerie, filtering the light from above, casting the great hall in a premature dusk.

Krýl again looked to Aílea, then to the squat man made of crystal. His golden eyes showed not the slightest hint of emotion.

"Come on."

"The animals—" began Aílea.

Krýl sighed and took her by the wrist.

They moved in a zig-zag through the menagerie, skirting glass boxes and gilded cages. As they passed Krýl struck at the glass or pried the tops off of the terrariums. In their wake they left a squirming, scuttling, leaping trail of fauna. Rodents, amphibians, lizards, and insects scattered before the smoke, moving away from the mounting flames.

As Krýl pulled her along, Aílea raised her head, scented the air. "The primates? Have they…?"

Krýl peered back over his shoulder. "No."

A spined reptile, its whip-like tail trailing out behind it, overtook Krýl and the others. It darted for the shadows at the menagerie's far corner, making for the door. Before it could disappear beneath the archway a booted foot descended from out of the shadows, grinding it into the stones.

Krýl drew up short, Aílea stumbling into his back. She clutched at his shoulder to keep her balance. From behind Krýl could hear the sound of the crystalline deviant moving to catch up.

Naked steel followed the booted foot, a curved blade that shone bright even in the dim light. Next came Kaalah, his face drawn, his cheeks sunken, his eyes like pools of molten stone. Soot stained his forehead, his tunic, his armor. There were scorch marks on his sleeves.

Krýl took several steps forward. Aílea followed, both hands clutching his elbow.

Behind the captain trailed a dozen lancers, the same elites who had raided the caravan Krýl had been hired to protect what seemed like a lifetime ago. They too held scimitars or short spears. All had scaled breastplates, their heads wrapped in close-fitting turbans, their faces covered by veils of glistening mail. In their eyes Krýl saw men who were prepared to give their lives. They would not run from him, from the symbiote. They would drag him to his death even as he cut them down.

"Despoiler!" bellowed Kaalah, raising his sword and pointing it at Krýl's chest.

Krýl shook Aílea from his arm. She staggered backwards until she struck one of the last unopened enclosures. Within something squirmed and shook, kicking up a fan of sand. Clutching at the glass box Aílea moved her head back and forth, listening, her tongue darting in and out of her mouth. Beside her the crystalline deviant ground to a halt and squatted, motionless.

"She gave you everything!"

Krýl watched Kaalah advance, the point of his sword

139

steady despite an obvious hitch and roll in his step. Behind him the lancers matched his stride.

"She gave you the finest foods, the rarest of wines. She took you to her bed, shared with you the wonders of her collections. You repay her with fire and slaughter!"

Krýl's shoulders hunched and the armor twitched. "She gave me a chance to die in that wonderful collection of hers."

Kaalah spat to one side. "You've burned treasures that can never be replaced. Whole archives have been consumed, artifacts and art all melted to slag!"

Spines grew from Krýl's shoulders, elbows, knees, and knuckles. They were joined by blades from his wrists and tendrils from his back.

"She spent lifetimes gathering these things so that they would not be lost to the ages. And in one day, one single day, you've undone generations of work!"

It was true.

Beneath his faceplate Krýl felt his mouth turn down at the corners.

"Maybe you'd be happy as a part of her collection, but I will not be consigned to some hall of curios."

"You are nothing!" bellowed Kaalah. "Do you hear me? You are nothing! Nothing!"

Kaalah managed two more strides before Krýl dove at him. He was met by a wall of steel and flesh.

The lancers poured around Kaalah, dog-piling Krýl as he flung himself forwards. In a heap they tumbled backwards, their momentum spilling them onto the floor in a jumble of limbs and fountaining arteries. As Krýl kicked men aside the armor drank in the slaughter.

Swords beat at Krýl's head, joints, and sides. Steel rang as the armor shrugged off the blows, the carapace growing harder with each drop of blood, each morsel of flesh it consumed.

Grappling with Krýl's outstretched claws, one of the lancers seized his wrists. The man's fingers and palms ran red as the spiked surface of the armor cut him to the bone. Krýl forced the lancer to his knees, grasped either side of his head, and pressing his barbed thumbs into the man's eyes. The soldier shrieked while his comrades hacked at Krýl's back, their swords striking sparks from his flanks. He paid them no mind, allowing the armor to focus on drinking before letting the corpse drop.

Another of the lancers leapt on his back trying to force Krýl down beneath his weight. Lashing tendrils vivisected the man, taking him apart even as he tried to maintain his grip. Krýl felt the pieces fall away, one after the other.

Krýl roared, swung, felt flesh and bone yield to bladed excursions. Beneath his heel a man's skull burst. To his left another lost his lower jaw. To his right yet another lost both hands at the wrists.

More lancers piled in, then more. Krýl killed them, pushed them back and back until pain blossomed along his side. He staggered then, falling back from the fray. Where the edge of a poisoned scimitar had cut into his ribs the armor was beginning to blacken and peel.

Krýl ducked another sword stroke, then kicked in the knee of the lancer who had swung the blade. The soldier crumpled.

Looking down at his injured side Krýl cursed. The toxin decayed the carapace at an astonishing rate, bits of it falling to the floor to join with the ash, and soot, and blood.

Another lancer rushed him and another lancer died. He sunk his fingers into the man's throat and let the armor drink. Again Krýl looked down. As he watched the carapace rebuilt itself, the abundance of flesh, and blood, and bone allowing it to outpace the poison.

Krýl relieved the nearest lancer of his head, then drove his blade into the next man's midriff. Metal scales fell away and went skittering across the flagging. Krýl lifted the lancer then hurled him at the others sending them sprawling.

From somewhere behind the wall of soldiers Krýl could hear Kaalah barking orders. The lancers responded silently, advancing without compunction or dubiety. A new wave of the lancers surged over the bodies of their comrades, hacking at the armor's tendrils with poisoned blades. Each new tendril that sprouted was cut away, their ends blackened. At last Krýl was reduced to striking only at arm's length. He parried, thrust, gouged, cut. Chitin rang against steel. Blades shattered, men fell from him screaming. Krýl moved like a dervish, a blur of serrated edges and ancient, ancient craving.

The last of the lancers to die did so silently, choking on his own blood, both of Krýl's blades shoved to the wrists in his chest. When the armor had drink its fill he let the body fall.

Shoulders hunched Krýl stood atop the heaped remains of the Witch's guard. Below him, sword held in a white-knuckled hand, was a single man.

"Kaalah."

The guardsman clutched a wound in his thigh, a deep gash that sent a dark stain down the white leg of his trousers. He glared at Krýl from out of bloodshot eyes.

"You…you are nothing…do you hear me?"

Krýl stepped from the mound of corpses.

"Nothing…"

Krýl toed a legless foot from his path, stepped over a head that lay face down in a puddle of red.

Kaalah spat to one side. "You have no reason to live other than to take, to destroy! You are as much a plague on this world as the crystal storms."

Krýl stopped. Kaalah met his eyes.

"The Witch said the same."

His gaze turned from Kalaah to the enclosure against which he had thrust Aílea. Within the glass case was the spined tangle of the sandwurm, its head upraised. Like a four-petaled flower lined with rows of needle-like teeth its mouth hung open, ropes of spittle dangling from its jaws.

Turning back to Kaalah, Krýl struck the glass with the side of his fist.

The sandwurm struck like an adder.

Latching its mouth around Kaalah's face the creature drove the guardsman to the floor. There it wrapped itself around him, squeezing, twisting, grinding. There was a pause as it constricted, then blood burst from the spaces between the armored coils.

As the wurm rolled over and over on itself Krýl watched as one soot-blackened hand was turned in a complete circle. When at last the wrist went limp and the clutching fingers relaxed he turned away.

"Aílea…"

The deviant woman was gone, no longer hidden in the shadow of the wurm's enclosure.

"Aílea!"

From behind a heap of lancers Krýl heard a moan, a gurgling intake of breath.

Krýl mounted the pile of dead, slid down the opposite side, and fell to his knees.

She lay sprawled on her back, her eyes moving from side to side. Her left breast, her belly, her right side were cut through, lashed as if by a razor. Blood ran in rivulets over her scales, a stain of carmine on white. Pinning her to the ground was a soldier, half of his torso cut away. On his back sat one of the blue and yellow frogs, its mouth cocked in a knowing little smile. Krýl drew back his hand, the armor warning him to keep away.

The small animal croaked once, then fell silent.

Aílea gasped, blood running from the corners of her mouth. She stirred, tried to lift herself, then fell back. To this the frog took umbrage and hopped away.

Even as the armor protested, Krýl raised his hand. Crawling forward he touched Aílea on the shoulder. She did not move. Krýl prodded her again. Still, there was nothing. Lifting the dead lancer from atop her, Krýl pulled her in close.

Holding Aílea to his chest, he gently rocked her while around him the flames began to sweep through the enclosures. The conflagration moved from one case to the next, consuming the rare plants, the tiny environments they had once contained. Lifting his head Krýl listened to the roar of the flames, the pop of overheated glass, and the sound of stone grating on stone.

Krýl watched as the crystalline deviant trundled past. It spared him a single glance, then turned towards the capering shadows on the far side of the menagerie. Slipping beneath the archway it was gone. A moment later it was followed by the primates. Leaping, bounding over the dead lancers, their palms and feet stained red, the small animals screeched and howled. Krýl watched them go then lowered his head, pressing Aílea's cheek to his own.

Four

The last of the daylight touched the upper walls of the keep, coruscating from the flecks of mica set in the red stones.

Those sections of the wall that had already been touched by fire were muted, stained black as pitch. Overhead great columns of smoke rose into the hot air. They towered over the valley, twisting, changing. Krýl watched as they drifted languidly to the north. At the base of the columns he could see a mounting yellow-orange glow. From this distance it appeared sickly, jaundiced.

As he looked on a column of flame burst from the highest of the towers.

Between the walls of the keep and Krýl's vantage stood the gardens. Most had been spared, but the closest beds and greenhouses had succumbed, burned or withered by the advancing flames. Interspersed with the surviving foliage were the mangled stumps of the Witch's pods. Their contents were strewn across the ground, now little more than carrion left to rot in the sun.

In each of the pods there had been a different woman, a body that varied in both shape and size. Some looked almost human; others were strange, alien, perhaps deviants or forced mutations. Some were tall and thin, some were plump and curved, but all were possessed of the preternatural beauty that had been the Witch's hallmark.

Krýl surveyed the keep, the flames, the gardens, the pods. He traced his own progress through the Witch's domain. What he saw staggered him.

From somewhere in the depths of the keep there came a muffled report. The sound rolled away over the plateau. A moment later and it was followed by another plume of smoke.

A hand on his arm made Krýl turn. Looking down he saw the crystalline deviant peering up at him, its golden eyes catching the light of the setting sun. The deviant removed its hand and pointed to the desert. Krýl looked in the direction it had indicated and nodded. The crystalline deviant lowered its hand and moved slowly off into the gathering shadows.

Krýl returned his attention to the fortress.

The tallest of the towers had turned black, the edges of the stonework glowing molten and red. As he watched, the roof caved in taking with it the upper battlements. They seemed to fall in slow motion, floating like scattered feathers towards the courtyard below. When the crash and rumble finally reached Krýl's ears it sounded small and forlorn.

Coaxing the eukaryotic shell from his head and hands Krýl rubbed one palm over his scalp. The sun had slipped behind the mountains and the fire-blackened walls were now in shadow. Soon there would be nothing to see but dying embers.

Krýl put his back to the keep, the gardens, the pods… Aílea. He took several steps towards the mountains, then pulled up short. A section of the gathering dusk detached itself from the rest of the shadows and moved towards him.

Krýl waited until the Shade was nearly upon him, then struck at it. His blow passed through the creature's head.

The Shade stood silently and still, a hazy absence of light that was both as real and as transient as flame. Through its head, its torso, its arms and legs the remains of the Witch's garden shimmered.

Krýl frowned. "What do you want?"

For a moment the Shade did not answer. Krýl began to grow impatient. Along his back and sides the eukaryotic shell rippled.

"I have what I want."

"Then why are you here?"

Again the Shade was silent. Krýl turned to go.

"The Witch…"

Krýl looked back over his shoulder. "The Witch?"

"Yes."

"What about her?"

"Where is she?"

Krýl shrugged. "How would I know? By now she's most likely dead, buried."

The Shade slipped forward. Krýl took a step back.

"You did not see her…die?"

Krýl shook his head.

"Then where?"

"I don't know."

The Shade considered this for a moment then said, "You should have killed her, fed her to the flames."

Krýl's frown turned itself into a snarl. "You used me!"

"I gave you the truth."

Krýl considered lashing out at the Shade with one of the armor's tendrils then banished the idea. It would do him no more good than trying to hammer the insubstantial thing with his fist. "You sent me into her greenhouse, led me to that heap of slime and snails."

The outline of the Shade blurred as if a wind on the other side of reality had tugged it out of shape.

"You saw what she truly was."

Krýl glowered at the Shade. "Because of you everything is in ruins."

"By your hand," said the Shade, "not mine."

The crack of more stones falling from the walls drifted through the gloaming. Krýl winced. "Why? Why did you send me to the Witch's greenhouse? Why did you direct me to that offal pit?"

For an instant it seemed as though the Shade might be laughing. As it snapped back into shape it said, "I needed an instrument."

"An instrument?"

"This is my home," said the Shade, "not hers. Not truly. It has been my home since before the sun turned red and burned the land. It is now mine again."

"That's it? You're upset because you think she took the keep from you?"

"It has been restored to me."

Krýl spat. "All of this...this ruin?"

"Yes."

"Because you felt displaced?"

"It is my home."

"Why bother telling me this?"

The Shade turned its head and regarded Krýl. "Tell all you meet who is truly master here. Tell them I will not brook interlopers."

For a moment there was silence, then Krýl began to laugh. "It doesn't matter what you will or will not brook! Men will come to this valley by the hundreds. They'll see the smoke; they'll know the Witch is gone. It will mean war for mastery of the keep. You'll have more company than ever before. My friend, you were better off with the Witch!"

The Shade hunched up its shoulders and hissed.

Krýl stopped laughing and raised his chin. "For a moment I considered making a claim to this place."

The Shade crouched low, hooked its fingers into claws. "You would not dare!"

"It was a stupid idea." Krýl gestured towards the open desert. "I belong out there, not shut inside the blackened walls of a dead keep. But fear not, there will be others."

"No!" The Shade's voice was strained, thin, a wisp of acrid smoke. "No, this place is mine! She took it from me!"

Krýl shrugged. "She took it and she filled it with all sorts of things, ancient things. She cultivated gardens and sheltered animals. She preserved where others sought only to destroy."

"She was a thief!"

"She was also a butcher and a torturer, a collector of sentient species that she treated as no more than chattel. She's gone now. We are free, you and I."

"Yes," said the Shade. "Free…"

"I doubt if you'll care much for what will be visited upon you in the Witch's stead."

"No!" cried the Shade, its outline bursting like a drop of ink in water. "I will not have it!"

With a snort Krýl turned his back on the Shade. He moved slowly into the darkness, away from the remains of the keep, the gardens. Behind him the flames continued to rise.

EPILOGUE

———•●•———

Jórn strained. Jórn lifted. Jórn heaved. Slowly, slowly the slab of stone began to move. Adjusting his grip he redoubled his efforts. The stone rose, dust cascading from its sides. When it was at a right angle to the ground he let it drop.

Wiping at the sweat on his forehead Jórn stood and surveyed his handiwork. In the place where the fire blackened stone had been there was now a gaping hole. Even though the sun stood near its zenith the pit was as dark as midnight. Scratching at his beard Jórn peered within.

The floor of the chamber lay far, far below. Even the bar of sunlight that streamed through the opening he had made dimmed towards its bottom. Taking a rock in one hand, Jórn dropped it into the pit. He listened as it fell, counting the seconds. When it finally struck he whistled.

"What'd you find?"

Jórn raised his head. Tottering over the rubble to his right was a short, thin man. His nose was long and thin, his mouth pinched, his chin weak. Beneath the man's hood his eyes darted continuously back and forth.

"It's a hole." Jórn heard his words drop through the opening at his feet and echo through the blackness.

The thin man drew level with Jórn. "Is that all?"

Jórn stretched, his shoulders and elbows popping. The thin man cringed.

"It's a deep hole."

"Oh." The thin man turned to go.

"Nash."

"What?"

"There's something down there."

Turning back towards Jórn, the thin man shuffled to the edge of the pit. Daintily he peered into the dark and dust.

"And what, exactly, do you think you see down in that deep hole?"

Jórn shrugged. "Something…different."

"Different?"

Jórn nodded towards the expanse of fire-blackened rubble on which they stood. There were charred stones, heaps of slag, the occasional broken buttress. In the distance there were the remains of a defensive curtain, the hint of a tower or two. Wrack and ruin.

"Different," said Jórn.

Nash regarded him for a moment, ran his tongue over his teeth. "Different," he said at last. "Alright."

Putting his index and thumb in his mouth Nash gave a long, shrill whistle. The scattered cadre of men that wandered in the near distance looked up. Nash waved to one of them. "Bring the ropes! We've found something!"

"Slowly, now," said Jórn. "Slowly."

"You heard him," hissed Nash, "slow…real slow."

From the direction of the light there was a grunt and the rope slipped half a foot.

"Slow, you stupid bunch of cunts!"

From the mouth of the hole thirty feet above there came a muffled apology.

"Shit-bricks…"

Nash's epithet went drifting off into empty space, dying before it reached the far wall.

Jórn snorted.

"What?"

Jórn shook his head. "Nothing."

"Goddamn right, nothing."

Nash adjusted his grip on the rope, his belaying harness creaking beneath his weight.

Jórn looked back up towards the light. Peering at them were several faces, the features hidden in shadow. From beside him Nash directed another curse at the phantom onlookers. "Slow, you whoresons! I don't want to go sliding down this damned rope and splattering who knows how far below."

The rate of descent again decreased.

"You didn't have to come."

Nash snorted. "I did. Can't have you laying claim to everything you see once you're down there."

Jórn chuckled.

Together the two men hung in space, slowly inching downwards, their lives hanging by two lengths of braided hemp. Around them the blackness was broken only by the single bar of sunlight that shone through the aperture above. Motes of dust swam in the light, turning, twisting as the descending figures disturbed the air.

Nash's feet were the first to reach bottom. As his soles came to rest a cloud of dust rose from the floor. Nash coughed, wheezed, coughed some more. Fumbling in his pack he drew out a cloth and hastily tied it around his mouth and nose.

A moment later Jórn touched down beside him, a cloth wrapped about the lower half of his face.

"Could have saved your lungs some trouble, tied that thing on while we were still descending."

With his chest still hitching the thin man made an obscene gesture, then motioned for a torch. Jórn obliged. When the brand was lit and his cough had subsided, Nash raised the torch and peered about.

They stood ankle deep in ash and dust, the piles they had disturbed drifting just overhead. Visibility was limited to only a few feet in any direction.

Jórn lit a torch of his own. "Which way?"

"How am I supposed to know? You found this hole."

Jórn thought for a moment then began to move off through the ash, kicking it up as he went.

"Hey!"

Jórn stopped, turned. "What?"

"Wait for me."

Nash took a dozen steps towards Jórn, tripped, and fell. More ash swirled.

Jórn stalked back the way he had come, snagged Nash by the back of his tunic, and dragged him to his feet. With a curse Nash shook himself free.

"Caution," said Jórn, raising one finger. "We don't know what's under all that ash. There could be pitfalls, broken stones—"

Nash snapped his head around to glare at the larger man. "You don't think I know that?"

"If you fall to your death I'll lay claim to everything I find down here. Including whatever it was you just tripped over."

Nash's lip curled back from his teeth. "You can go to hell. I was the one that gathered those idiots above. I paid their wages. I got us to these ruins before anyone else. I have first claim on anything we find down here. Now, stop standing and smirking, you great lump of clay." Nash stopped and peered into Jórn's face. "Are you listening to me? What the hell is wrong with you?"

"Do you see that?"

Nash peered up at the bearded giant, his eyes narrowed to slits.

"There," said Jórn, pointing.

Nash turned around and scanned the darkness. "What? That thing?"

Jórn nodded.

"It's a rock."

"It's too smooth to be just a rock."

"That's because there's ash on it. Trust me, it's a rock."

Jórn pushed past the pinch-faced little man and disappeared into the swirling cloud of ash. The glow of his torch lingered for a moment then faded, leaving Nash alone with the sound of his own muffled breathing.

"It's a goddamn rock, that's all! It's not worth poking around in the dark…for…" Nash looked about himself, saw nothing but ash and the sickly orange glow of his own torch. Squinting into the darkness he slunk forward, straining to catch a glimpse of Jórn's torch.

"Jórn? Jórn I can't see a goddamn thing…Jórn?"

Nash tripped. Nash fell.

Again Jórn was there to haul him upright.

"Should watch were you walk."

"Ow," said Nash.

Jórn propped Nash on his own two feet, began to dust off the smaller man's tunic. Nash batted his hand away.

"Stop. Just stop!"

"Alright, I've stopped."

Glaring about himself Nash waved Jórn away then kicked at the thing that had tripped him. The toe of his boot contacted something firm, but pliable, not stone as he had expected. Bending down Nash peered at the thing.

"Is it a root?"

"Could be. This look like a plant to you?"

"What, like a…tree, or a bush, or something?" Nash stood and turned towards the object Jórn had indicated. "That's a rock. I already told you as much."

"It's not," said Jórn. "And the thing you tripped over, it looks more like a vein than a root."

"I know it's what tripped me!" spat Nash. "But a vein, that doesn't make any goddamned sense."

"Look closer."

Nash looked closer. The structure that ran along the floor did indeed resemble a vein. From its sides there extended tributaries that grew smaller as they spread. Where the ash had been disturbed its surface was covered in a pallid, fungal growth.

Nash kicked at the root, or vein, or whatever it was. The thing reacted, contracting as if aware it had been struck. The thin man balked.

"Did you see that? Did you bloody see that?"

"You kicked it," said Jórn. "I saw."

"I kicked it and it moved!"

"No," said Jórn, "you kicked it and that's why it moved."

Nash shook his head. "I'm going to go this way," he said, pointing back the way they had come. "I suggest you come too. There's nothing down here for us."

Jórn raised his torch. "I'm going to keep looking. You do

whatever it is you think you need to do."

Nash made a grab for Jórn's torch. Jórn simply raised his arm. The thin man's swing went wide.

"I'm going this way," said the big man, pointing towards the large shape.

"It's a rock, Goddamn it…"

"With a vein connected to it."

Jórn turned about and began to walk. Reluctantly Nash followed, puffs of ash rising around them as their feet stirred it from the floor. As it drifted upwards more lengths of the strange vein-like growths were revealed. With each step the protuberances seemed to grow closer together, heaping themselves one on top of the other. The footing became treacherous. Twice more Nash stumbled, each time catching himself just before he went sprawling. At last the dark and the unsteady footing got the better of him and Nash went down hard. Striking his chin on one of the protuberances he felt his teeth clack together. When he lifted his head he tasted blood.

"Stop! Goddamn it Jórn, just stop!"

Looking up he saw that the big man already had.

Jórn stood with his torch upraised. In the motes of ash that drifted about his head the brand guttered, sparked.

"What?" asked Nash, dragging himself to his feet yet again. "What do you see?"

The big man did not respond. He simply stood and stared at the shape from the darkness. Nash followed his gaze.

Its edges were split evenly, like the two halves of a seed pod. The top half had been pushed back, its underside dripping with a clear viscous fluid. The woman that stood at its center was tall, her hair a cascade of green that fell over her shoulders like liquid emeralds. Her skin was pale, the light of Jórn's torch passing through to touch upon the blood vessels and musculature beneath. Though she was thin, the woman's limbs seemed to radiate a tensile strength, as if she were woven of cordage that had been drawn taught. Even in the wan light the two men could see that her features were angular, almost severe. From sclera to iris her eyes were completely black. Unblinking, the woman glared out at the two men, her expression one of barely contained fury. At the sight of her they quailed.

"Kneel," said the Pellucid Witch in a voice like the desert wind. "Kneel and I may allow you to serve me."

ABOUT THE AUTHOR

Born in southern California in the early 1980's, Owen now lives in northern Colorado with his wife, their cats, and more books than he will ever be able to read. He has edited and contributed to eight volumes of the fantasy and horror anthology, 'Exterus', and the stand-alone fantasy anthology, 'Magissa'. He has written several other novels both under his own name and various pseudonyms.

Made in United States
Troutdale, OR
07/09/2025

32760562R00100